BOOK NINE IN THE LANDON SAGA

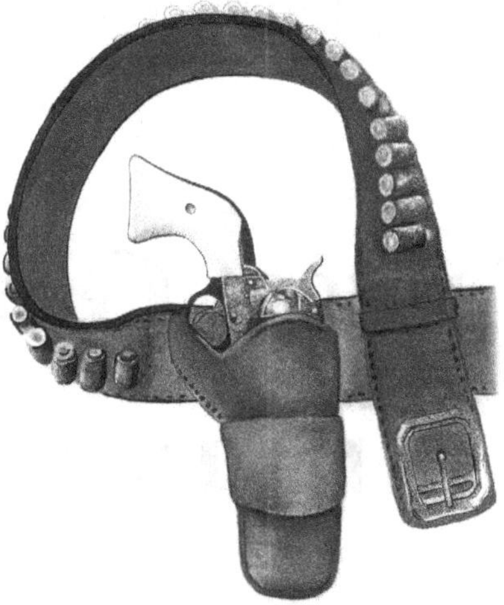

FASTEST GUN AROUND

A SOLSTICE WESTERN

TELL COTTEN

Fastest Gun Around

Tell Cotten

The Landon Saga novels by Tell Cotten

Confessions of a Gunfighter
Entwined Paths
Cooper
Rondo
Yancy
Lee
They Rode Together
Warpath
Fastest Gun Around

Also by Tell Cotten
Wanted: A Western Story Collection
(Includes The Mirror, a Landon Saga short story)

Dedication
To my sister-in-law, Beth; thanks for the proofreads!

Illustrator: Bill Olivas
www.billolivas.com
wbolivas@yahoo.com

Cover Art:
Marcy Meinke/Converse Printing & Design
www.ConversePrinting.com
mike@converseprinting.com

Publisher's Note:

This is a work of fiction. All names, characters, places, and
events are the work of the author's imagination.

Any resemblance to real persons, places, or events is
coincidental.

Solstice Publishing - www.solsticepublishing.com

While FASTEST GUN AROUND can be read as a stand alone, it is recommended that new readers start with the first book in the series, CONFESSIONS OF A GUNFIGHTER.

The Landon Saga currently has five main characters that interact through the novels. For a quick reminder, below is the recent status of each main character.

Rondo Landon: Married to Rachel, Mr. Tomlin's daughter. Rondo is an ex-outlaw and lawman, now working for J.T. Tussle as a ranch hand.

Yancy Landon: Cousin to Rondo. Newly appointed as a Texas Ranger, and is romantically involved with Jessica Tussle, who is J.T. Tussle's niece.

Cooper Landon: Cousin to Rondo, and Yancy's older brother. Married to Josie, and has an adopted son, Wyatt, who was rescued from the Apaches. Like Yancy, he is also a newly appointed Texas Ranger.

Lee Mattingly: An ex-outlaw, and a friend of Rondo's. Romantically involved with April Gibson. He also owns part interest in the Palace Hotel, along with partner Brian Clark.

August 'Winchester' Landon: A cousin to Yancy, Cooper, and Rondo. Winchester is currently an Apache scout in the New Mexico Territory.

Part One
"A Week Earlier"

Chapter one

Ross Stewart sat on the porch at the jail. He was drinking coffee, studying a chessboard, and watching the activity in the street.

It was early morning, and Empty-lake was just waking up. Town folks exchanged pleasantries as they walked by, on their way to their place of work.

Ross was the sheriff, and he was in his late twenties. He had a tall and lanky frame, with tanned skin and brown hair. When he spoke he always displayed a rich, Texas drawl.

Empty-lake was mostly a cow town of some two-dozen buildings. Two establishments stood out the most; the sheriff's office built by the late Lieutenant Porter, and the Palace Hotel.

The hotel was the tallest building in town, and it could be seen from all directions. There was a fancy porch, a fresh paint job, and numerous windows.

The jail also had a porch and windows that lined the front. There were living quarters in a side room beside the office, and in the back were six well-built cells.

Ross sighed and stretched. The early morning sun felt good, and he was in no hurry to go anywhere.

He took a swig of coffee and wiped his mouth with his shirtsleeve. As he lowered his hand, he glanced up the street and spotted two riders. They rode with purpose, and Ross's curiosity was kindled.

The man in the lead was an older man. Ross figured he was in his sixties, but he still had a spry and collected look. He was thin, tall, and lanky. He had sharp, narrow eyes, and a white beard. There was also the suggestion of lost handsomeness in his face.

His companion was much younger, perhaps in his late twenties. He had a hard, chip-on-the-shoulder expression.

He was lean, hard-bodied, and short. He displayed a Colt on his hip, and it looked like he knew how to use it.

Ross straightened in his chair, and he lowered his gun hand so that it hovered naturally over his Colt's handle.

The riders spotted him and rode over. They pulled up, and it was silent for several seconds. The younger one displayed an arrogant smirk, but the older one studied Ross with a professional carefulness.

"Just rode into town," he said in a clear, surprisingly gentle voice.

"I see that," Ross said.

"You the sheriff?"

"I am."

The older man nodded and gazed up the street.

"Elegant hotel," he gestured with his head.

"Is," Ross agreed.

"Who owns it?"

"That's a complicated question," Ross said wryly. "Right now, a fella named Ed Hazel does. And some others, I think."

"Changes ownership regularly, eh?"

"You could say that."

The older man nodded, and Ross was quiet as he waited for the conversation to go to another place.

"Searching for a feller," the older man finally said. "Heard he was here."

"Oh? Who?"

"Rondo Landon," he announced, and Ross jumped in his chair. "I reckon you've heard of him," he added as he noticed Ross's reaction.

"We know each other," Ross acknowledged, and asked, "What's your business with him?"

"It's personal," he replied, and there was a warning in his voice that suggested Ross not ask anymore questions.

Ross nodded slowly. Nobody spoke, and the older man frowned his displeasure.

"Well, is Rondo here or not?"

"Was," Ross replied. "But not now."

The older man looked displeased.

"Where'd he go?"

"New Mexico Territory. Something to do with his wife."

"When will he be back?"

"He didn't say," Ross said, not wanting to give out too much information.

The older man looked at Ross a moment.

Then he said, "You don't talk much."

"Only when I have something to say," Ross forced a smile.

The older man mumbled under his breath and looked back at the hotel. Meanwhile, Ross took advantage of the silence and pried for some information.

"I've never seen you around here."

He grunted.

"That's cause I've never *been* here."

Ross nodded and asked, "Long ways from home?"

"Long enough."

"Plan on staying long?"

"Haven't decided."

"I see," Ross said, and added, "This is a peaceful little town. We don't tolerate any trouble."

The older man looked amused.

"We?"

"I meant me," Ross said, and his face turned slightly red.

"What's your name?" He suddenly looked interested.

Ross told him.

"Never heard of you."

"Most haven't."

"Any good with that?" He gestured at the Colt on Ross's hip.

"I've been good enough."

The older man gave a knowing smile.

10

"Perhaps we'll see," he said, and his companion snickered.

"What do you mean?" Ross narrowed his eyes.

"Just that."

He kicked up his horse as soon as he said that, and his companion followed him down the street. They pulled up at the livery stable and dismounted.

Ross looked thoughtful as he watched them.

"Trouble," he said to himself. He thought on that, and added softly, "I wish Rondo *was* here."

Chapter two

Ross was the curious sort, and he watched as the newcomers led their horses inside the livery stable.

He had never seen the older man; that he was sure. However, the youngest looked familiar. But, try as he might, he couldn't recall when or where he'd seen him.

Ross was troubled.

He knew a day like this would arrive someday. Before, he had always depended on the Landons or Lee Mattingly for help. But they weren't here, and he was alone.

He was adequate with a Colt. But still, his skill just didn't compare to Rondo and others.

Ross understood his limitations. It was a worrisome burden, because the town folks looked to him for protection.

He could never admit that he doubted his ability. Not even to Rondo. After all, *he* was the sheriff, and folks expected him to have all the answers.

There was one thing Ross didn't lack, and that was his willingness. He wouldn't run from a fight, no matter the odds.

He hoped when the time arrived, that would make up the difference.

***

The afternoon passed slowly, and Ross's uneasiness grew with each hour.

He kept himself busy at the jail. He swept the office, cleaned the jail cells, and sorted through papers on his desk.

Darkness finally arrived, but Ross wasn't hungry. Instead of supper, he built a fire in the stove and made some coffee.

He sat at his desk and drank a cup. The coffee was strong and black, and that's how he liked it.

He had just refilled his cup when the door burst open, and the bartender from the Palace Hotel rushed in.

Ross was startled, and he spilled coffee on his desk. He grabbed a towel and scowled as he wiped it up.

"Yes? What is it?"

"Trouble," the bartender said breathlessly. "Ed told me to fetch you."

"What sorta trouble?"

"Two strangers got a room this afternoon. One of them's playing poker and is losing big. He's drunk, and getting irritable."

"Which one is it?"

"The young one."

"Where is the other one?"

"We haven't seen *him* since they checked in."

Ross looked thoughtful and nodded.

"All right," he said. "I'll be along."

The bartender nodded and headed toward the door.

"I'll tell Ed."

"You do that."

"And hurry!" The bartender added.

Chapter three

Ross drained his cup of coffee with one swig. He stood, drew his Colt, and checked to make sure it was loaded.

He already knew it was, but it was reassuring to see the bullets.

He holstered the Colt, grabbed his hat, walked to the door, and stepped out.

His heart thumped as he walked down the street. His legs felt heavy and trembled slightly in anticipation.

Morgan McCann, a member of the town council, hurried over as Ross reached the hotel.

"Where've you been?" He demanded. "There's trouble in there."

"I heard."

"Can you handle this?"

Ross stopped and looked directly at Morgan.

"You think I can't?"

"I didn't say that," Morgan looked offended. "But, you don't have any help. You're all alone."

"Very observant," Ross said wryly. He raised an eyebrow and asked, "You offering?"

"Offering what?"

"To help."

"Listen; I'm just a concerned citizen. That's all."

"I appreciate your support," Ross said flatly.

Morgan frowned while Ross stepped up onto the porch.

"Ross," Morgan said, his voice somber.

"Yes?" Ross paused.

"I'll be at the door. If it comes to it, I'll back you up best as I can."

He seemed sincere, and Ross pinched his face in thought.

Morgan was the owner of a local saloon. He was no gunfighter, but he was big and muscled, and he'd thrown out his share of drunks.

"All right," Ross decided, "You're hired."

"After this, we're getting you a deputy," Morgan grumbled.

"That'd be helpful," Ross agreed, and asked, "Is your six-shooter loaded?"

Morgan palmed his Colt, opened the cylinder, and spun it.

"It is," he confirmed as he holstered it.

"Don't shoot unless you have to."

"I won't."

Ross nodded.

"Well, here goes," he said.

Morgan returned the nod, and Ross walked to the entrance. He breathed deeply, gathered himself, and pushed through the batwing doors.

Chapter four

Ross paused and allowed his eyes to adjust. Seconds later, Morgan came in and moved off to the side.

Ross took in the view, and once again he was impressed at how fancy and elegant the inside always seemed to look.

The hotel had two floors.

The hotel rooms were upstairs, and there was a balcony that circled three sides of the hotel. All of the rooms upstairs opened up from the balcony.

The restaurant and poker room were downstairs.

Along the length of one wall was an elaborate mahogany bar with a huge, fancy mirror behind it. Bottles and glasses were stacked behind the bar in decorative pyramids.

Along the other wall were a few gaming tables, and behind that was the poker room. In the middle of the room were some tables and chairs, and there was also a fancy chandelier hanging from the ceiling that, when lit, would light up the entire room.

Against the back wall was a fancy spiral staircase that split in two directions. There was a door underneath the stairs that led to the office.

A loud, angry voice could be heard from the poker room, and everyone looked concerned.

"About time he showed up," Ross heard a customer grumble.

Ross walked slowly towards the poker room. His heart thumped, and he wondered briefly how noticeable his trembling legs were.

He paused at the doorway and looked in.

The poker room was mostly empty, except for the main table. Four men were seated around it, but the young stranger was standing, sneering down at them.

Ed Hazel, the owner of the hotel, was one of the ones sitting. His hands were on the table, and he looked calm as he attempted to converse with the irritated stranger.

Ed was dark headed with a thin and frail frame. He had quick, shifty eyes, and he also had large upper teeth that showed most of the time.

Nobody knew where Ed had come from; he just showed up one day with plenty of money. There was talk about him being involved with Ike Nash, but it was only speculation.

"I want my money back!" The young stranger was saying, and there was hostility in his voice.

Ed spotted Ross in the corner of his eye, but he continued to give the young stranger his full attention.

"You're upset," he replied, and his voice almost sounded apologetic. "But, the fault is yours, not mine."

"How's that?" The young stranger glared at him.

"You're a very impatient poker player."

"You cheated!"

"No," Ed corrected. "I did not."

"Stand up," the young stranger said viciously.

Ed remained seated and glanced at Ross.

"Sheriff," he said, "this young man is obviously drunk. I suggest you lock him up and let him sleep it off."

All eyes went to Ross, and he tried his best to look mean.

"I appreciate the suggestion," Ross said gruffly. "I'll handle this."

"Please do," Ed smiled pleasantly.

The young stranger turned from the table, and an ugly sneer split his lips.

"Well now. If it ain't the sheriff."

"You're coming with me," Ross said forcefully.

He laughed at that, but not humorously.

"You arresting me?"

"I am," Ross demanded, and added, "Unbuckle your gun belt."

"I won't, and you can't make me."

"What makes you think that?" Ross frowned.

"My father. He's standing behind you."

Ross felt a sudden panic, but he managed to appear calm.

"You're bluffing."

"No," a familiar, gentle voice said from behind, "he's not."

Ross's eyes grew wide, and the young stranger's sneer turned into a nasty grin.

Chapter five

Ross stood rigid, and he could feel sweat forming on his forehead.

Several seconds passed. Nobody moved, and nobody spoke.

For a split second, Ross wondered why he was the sheriff. The thought of being a cowpuncher again had never been so appealing.

"You're between a rock and a hard place, Sheriff," the gentle voice from behind said.

Ross licked his lips but didn't reply.

"However, I've never enjoyed killing a man when it wasn't necessary."

"I'll agree with that," Ross said, relieved to hear it.

"There's no need for trouble. Just turn around, real slow like, and go back to the jail. I'll take care of my son."

Ross felt a strong urge to sprint towards the door, but he didn't allow himself to.

"I can't," he said.

"Why not?" The gentle voice sounded surprised.

"I've got a job to do. It's my responsibility."

"Don't be foolish."

Several tense seconds passed before Ross replied. He swallowed hard, prayed that Morgan would back him, and looked back at the young stranger.

"You're under arrest," he said in a curt voice. "Unbuckle your gun belt and stand back."

The young stranger stared disbelievingly at him.

"You're crazy," he muttered.

"I won't argue with that," Ross said.

The young stranger's face turned vicious, and his eyes narrowed. Nobody spoke, and the tension was thick.

Then the young stranger laughed.

"You're a dead man," he hissed, and grabbed for his Colt.

Chapter six

The young stranger was fast. But, this time, Ross was faster.

As Ross palmed his Colt, he knew he'd won. But, right before he fired, there was an explosion behind him, and a violent blast hit him in his shoulder. It spun him around, and his bullet hit the wall.

Meanwhile, the young stranger brought up his Colt and fired.

Ross felt another burning sensation hit his gun hand. His Colt went flying through the air, and Ross collapsed.

His head was spinning, and he lost all sense of direction. He mumbled a few words and kicked out. He tried to move, but nothing worked for him.

The older man walked over. With an ugly snarl, he pointed his Colt at Ross and started to pull the trigger.

"I wouldn't do that," a voice from behind said.

He turned around slowly. A big, muscled man at the door held a gun on him, and the bartender also covered him with a double-barreled shotgun.

He remained still as he eyed them.

"Take it easy now," he said, his voice gentle.

"Drop your guns," the man at the door said. "Both of you."

The older man shook his head slowly.

"Can't do that," he said.

"We'll shoot," the man at the door warned.

"I don't think you will," the older man replied, and asked, "You ever kill a man this close? It's not pleasant."

Nobody replied, and the older man smiled knowingly.

"We're walking out of here, real peaceful like," he said. "Then, we'll saddle our horses and leave."

"You just shot a man in the back," the man at the door objected.

"I was protecting my son. You can't blame a father for doing that. Besides, you're not a lawman. It's not your concern."

"Maybe not. But this is my town, and you were wrong."

"Morgan," the bartender spoke, his voice urgent. "Let them leave. We don't want anymore bloodshed."

Morgan didn't like it, and several tense seconds passed.

"Morgan," the bartender said again, his voice blunt. "Let them go."

Morgan frowned his displeasure, but he still nodded slightly and moved from the door.

The older man smiled.

"Let's go," he told his son.

"My money," the young stranger protested.

"Not now," he replied, his voice curt.

The young stranger looked sullen. He followed his father to the door while Morgan and the bartender covered them.

The older man paused at the door and looked at Ed Hazel, who had followed them to the main room.

"This ain't over," he vowed.

Then they stepped outside.

Chapter seven

Morgan stood by the window and kept watch. Meanwhile, the bartender sighed in relief and lowered his shotgun.

"I've got to load this thing one of these days," he complained. "Keeps slipping my mind."

Morgan shot the bartender a dark look.

"You mean-?"

"Why else would I have been so persistent to let 'em go?" The bartender objected.

Morgan grunted his disgust and looked back out the window. Meanwhile, Ed just stood there, his hands on his hips, and glared at his employee.

Ed started to say something, but Ross groaned before he could.

It was a loud and painful sound. Ross was on his back, clutching his hand, and was barely conscious.

"Somebody had best fetch the doctor for our brave sheriff," Ed said wryly.

"I'll go," the bartender offered.

"You do that," Ed said, and the bartender took off.

"At least he's good for something," Ed muttered, and he bent over and squinted at Ross's hand. "How 'bout that. They shot Ross's thumb off."

"They're riding out," Morgan suddenly announced from the window.

"For now," Ed said as he straightened back up. "You heard what he said, 'bout it not being over."

"So?" Morgan asked.

"He'll be back, and we don't have any law to protect us."

"We can worry about that later," Morgan said as he left the window.

Ed scowled, but Morgan ignored him as he knelt beside Ross.

"You all right?" He asked.

"Hurts," Ross whispered.

"Doc's on his way."

"How's my thumb?" Ross's voice was weak.

Morgan looked thoughtful as he glanced around.

"I'll let you know when we find it," he said.

Ross blinked at that. He managed to groan, and darkness closed in around him as he passed out.

Part Two
"A Week Later"

Chapter eight

We were covered in dust, saddle worn, and in need of a bath and shave. But, nobody seemed to care much.

We were at Mr. Tomlin's ranch headquarters. It was suppertime, and everyone was seated around the dinner table.

As always, the Tomlin's ranch headquarters was impressive. The main house was long and big, and the pole corrals were well kept and in good shape, as was the barn and bunkhouse.

We had ridden in only a few hours before. We brought good news with us, and it had been a festive afternoon.

Several weeks back, Apaches captured my wife, Rachel, and April Gibson.

I was devastated, and we took out after them with grim determination. Our chances were slim, but God was on our side. With the help of my cousin, Winchester, we recovered the girls.

Our success didn't come without consequences. Jeremiah Wisdom took a bullet in the gut, and he gave his life so we could escape.

Once we were out of danger, my cousins Yancy and Cooper bid us farewell. They rode northwest toward Midway while Winchester headed for the nearest army outpost to make his report.

The rest of us traveled here.

The Tomlins were anxious for news of their daughter, and I'll never forget the joyous looks on everybody's faces. It was a proud moment, and I felt a flood of emotion as I watched them embrace.

I was still feeling grand as I looked around the dinner table. Everyone present was considered a good friend, and I suddenly realized how lucky I was.

Mr. Tomlin sat at the head of the table. He was in his late fifties, and had lived a full life. He had white hair, and his face was weathered and wrinkled. But his eyes were clear and sharp, and he never seemed to miss a thing.

Beside him was the young ranch-hand Rory Wheeler, and next was Buster with his bum leg.

Then there was Brian Clark.

An ex-outlaw, Brian was a grizzled veteran in his mid-fifties. He was loyal, and he had a gentle-like way about him. He was always careful; he never took any chances unless he had to.

Recently, Brian had formed a partnership of sorts with Lee Mattingly, who was sitting across the table.

They were the owners of the Palace Hotel, and they also had a partner that they hadn't even met yet.

Lee was an ex-outlaw in his mid-thirties. He had a gentleman way about him, and he had a different set of ethics than most. He was soft spoken, and was loyal to those he considered friends.

He was also very good with a Colt, and he had the reputation to go with it.

Over the past few years, an unspoken friendship had sprouted between Lee and me. There was always a struggle going on inside Lee between right and wrong, and I knew all too well how that felt.

April Gibson sat beside Lee, looking proud and blissful.

She was a tall, graceful looking woman with tired eyes and a wisp of natural gray hair here and there. She was in her early thirties.

It was no secret that she had strong feelings for Lee. And, the feeling seemed mutual.

Next was April's daughter, June, who was now eleven. She had long, blond hair, round blue eyes, and a small, shapely face.

Beside her was my lovely wife, Rachel, who was in her early twenties. She had long, brown hair with sandy looking freckles that covered her face. She also had a knowing smile that always made me squirm.

And then there was me, Rondo Landon.

I was an ex-outlaw and sheriff, and I was also known as the man who killed Ben Kinrich. I wasn't proud of that, but it had to be done.

I was in my early twenties. I was small and hard bodied, with narrow hips and wide shoulders. I also displayed my well-known ivory-handled Colt on my right hip.

Mr. Tomlin interrupted my thoughts. He stood and smiled at his wife, who was a jovial and good-natured woman.

"There's a lot to be thankful for this day," he said, and everyone nodded their agreement. "Let's give thanks," he suggested.

We bowed our heads, and Mr. Tomlin said a long, appreciative prayer.

Before we ate, I stood and got everyone's attention. I held my drink high and cleared my throat.

"To Jeremiah Wisdom," I said, my voice somber.

Everyone looked subdued, and we toasted Jeremiah in silence. I noticed a quick tear roll down April's face.

"A good man," Lee said softly.

"Yes," Brian agreed. "He was."

I sat back down, and we ate whole-heartedly.

It was the best meal we'd had in weeks. This was also our first chance to relax, and everybody kidded around with each other.

We had some apple pie for dessert. As I took my last bite, Mr. Tomlin looked up suddenly.

"With all the excitement, I forgot to mention Ross," he said.

I smiled with the memory of another good friend.

"What's Ross up to?" I asked.

"He was shot."

The mood sobered instantly.

"Did he live?" I asked, my face tense.

"Yes, but he's in bad shape. He was shot in the back, and he also lost his thumb."

I felt the all too familiar cold, killing feeling begin to build in the pit of my stomach. I narrowed my eyes and leaned forward.

"Tell me what happened," I said, my voice flat.

Chapter nine

I didn't say much for the rest of the evening. I just sat there, my face dark and pinched in thought.

Rachel looked concerned. Finally, she leaned over and murmured in my ear.

"Let's go outside."

I nodded. We stood, and I followed her out onto the porch.

The sounds of the night were loud. We sat beside each other, and neither one of us spoke. Rachel was smiling sweetly, but I hardly noticed.

"Lovely evening," she finally said.

"Did you say something?" I looked at her.

"Let it go, Rondo," she said, her voice firm. "You're not the sheriff anymore."

"Ross is my friend," I objected. "And-."

"You don't have many friends," she finished my sentence.

I frowned at her but didn't reply.

"You heard what Pa said," Rachel said. "It happened over a week ago, and the men that shot Ross haven't been seen since. There's no telling where they are now."

"I could find them."

"Promise me you won't."

"Can't do that," I scowled. "That's not how I am."

Rachel returned the scowl and said, "You're ruining this perfect moment."

"What's so perfect about it?"

"I'm trying to tell you something."

"All right," I said. "Tell me."

"But you're upset."

"That usually happens when a friend gets shot."

Rachel sighed, and we were silent a moment. She just sat there, her arms crossed, looking out into the darkness.

I studied her, sighed, and cleared my throat.

"All right," I said. "I won't go after them."

Rachel's face lit back up.

"You promise?"

"Sure."

"Thank you."

"Tussle's waiting for us anyway," I continued. "It's time we headed for Midway. We're long overdue."

Rachel looked anxious.

"We need to talk about that," she said.

"Oh?"

"I don't want you to take the job."

"What?" I raised an eyebrow. "Too late for that. He hired me over a month ago. You know that."

"I'm not sure I should make the trip," Rachel replied, and she bit her lower lip.

I stared at her for several seconds.

"Why not," I said, my voice flat.

She hesitated, then blurted, "It might not be best for the baby."

I felt like a mule kicked me in the gut. I couldn't breath, and I almost fell off the porch. Meanwhile, Rachel stared at me through wide eyes.

"What's wrong with you?" I heard a voice from behind.

I turned, and Lee, April, and June were walking out of the house.

"Nothing much," I managed.

"Lover's quarrel?" Lee smiled pleasantly.

I glared at him, and Lee's smile turned to a grin.

"We thought we'd take a stroll," he said.

"Don't let us stop you," I urged.

Lee's eyes twinkled. He glanced at Rachel, and then looked back at me.

"Good luck," he said.

I continued to glare at him, but Lee didn't seem to notice. They left the porch and disappeared into the darkness.

After that, Rachel and I just sat there. We didn't speak, and the silence was awkward.

Chapter ten

As soon as they left the porch, Lee Mattingly became nervous. He ambled along beside April, and June played in front of them.

He glanced sideways at April. She smiled encouragingly, and he smiled back awkwardly.

Say something, he scolded himself.

"Pleasant evening," he finally broke the silence.

"Yes," April replied. "Very."

Lee grinned like a fool and nodded. They walked a bit further, and he coughed and cleared his throat.

"Rondo and Rachel seemed to be having an intense conversation," he mused.

"They have a lot to discuss," April smiled knowingly.

"Oh?"

April hesitated, then asked, "Can you keep a secret?"

"Most of the time."

April lowered her voice so June couldn't hear.

"Rachel's going to have a baby."

Lee thought on that, and April was surprised when his face turned savage.

"Those Injun devils," he snarled.

"No, no," April corrected quickly. "Rondo and Rachel are having the baby."

Lee's face lit up.

"Rondo's going to be a father?"

"Yes."

Lee chuckled at the thought and said, "How 'bout that."

"Rachel is worried how he's going to take the news," April continued.

"He'll be surprised."

"I'm sure he will be."

"And, he'll worry," Lee continued. "He's like that."

"Worry about what?" April was curious.

"Everything," Lee grinned.

Chapter eleven

"You're having a baby," I finally broke the silence.

"*We* are, yes," Rachel replied.

"How long have you known?"

"A few days before I was captured."

I shook my head in wonder.

"Everything you endured with those Injuns, and you were pregnant the whole time," I said softly.

"I'm tough, I guess."

Suddenly, I had a deeper appreciation for my wife.

"Do your parents know?" I asked.

"I wanted to tell you first."

I nodded, and it was silent a moment. Rachel glanced at me, and she looked anxious.

"How do you feel?"

"Sorta numb," I admitted.

"But are you happy?"

"I think I am."

"But you're not overjoyed."

"Give me a moment for the surprise to wear off," I laughed shakily. "I didn't see this coming. That's all."

A thought suddenly occurred to me, and I glanced at her with concern.

"You should see a doctor."

"I was thinking the same thing," she agreed.

"Is something wrong?" Worry filled my face.

"No, not at all," Rachel reassured. "I'd just like to talk to him."

"I'll ride to town, first thing in the morning," I declared.

Rachel nodded, and her face turned wistful.

"There's something else I'd like to discuss," she said.

"What is it?"

"I'd like to have the baby here, with my family."

"We have family in Midway too," I reminded. "And when the baby comes, Josie could help."

Rachel scowled and said, "I think not. I've heard how she is."

I grinned sheepishly but didn't say anything.

"I'd feel more comfortable here," Rachel continued.

I nodded thoughtfully.

"I can understand that," I said, then added, "That means no job with Tussle."

"I'm afraid so."

"I'll also have to find a job around here."

"Pa would hire you," Rachel said quickly. "He'd be glad to."

"But we'd have no place to live," I pointed out.

Rachel had it all figured out, and she shook her head.

"The main house is plenty big," she said. "I'm sure my parents wouldn't mind."

I frowned at the thought.

"It might work, for a while," I said grudgingly.

"It's settled then?" Rachel looked hopeful.

"I guess, as long as your parents agree."

"Oh, they will!"

I nodded, and it was silent a moment.

"Tussle needs to know," I said suddenly.

"We could write," Rachel suggested.

"No," I shook my head. "I should tell him face to face. He deserves that."

Rachel wanted to protest, but she could tell I had made up my mind. So, she let it go.

"Long trip," she commented.

"I'll hurry."

"When will you leave?"

"Sooner the better," I said, and asked, "You need me here for any reason?"

"I guess not."

"I'll leave tomorrow then, after I fetch the doctor."

36

Rachel nodded, and I smiled as I looked at her.

"And Rachel," I said, my voice soft.

"Yes?"

"I'm happy. *Very* happy. It's just going to take some time to get used to the idea. That's all."

Rachel nodded and asked, "How long will you be gone?"

"Two, three weeks at the most."

"That should be plenty of time," Rachel smiled sweetly.

I smiled back and chuckled.

"I reckon so," I said.

Chapter twelve

Lee and April walked side by side.

Lee's hands were in his pockets, except for his thumbs, and he had a thoughtful look.

April waited for him to say something. Finally, she decided to help.

"What's on your mind?" She urged.

"I'd make a good father," Lee suddenly blurted, and his face turned slightly red.

April looked interested.

"You're fond of babies?"

"Not particularly," Lee admitted. "But I like children. Always have; I just haven't been around them much."

"I'll remember that."

It was silent a moment, and April glanced anxiously at Lee.

"So, what happens next?"

"Well, Rondo will have a lot to think about."

"I meant with us," April corrected.

"Oh," Lee looked startled.

April smiled and waited patiently while Lee collected his thoughts.

"I've made several promises lately," Lee finally said. "To you, June, and even Jeremiah."

"You have."

"I reckon it's time I started keeping my word."

"That'd be nice," April said, and added, "Which promise comes first?"

"I'm open to suggestions."

April nodded and gestured ahead at her daughter.

"You said you'd spend time with June."

"That's right. And I meant it."

"She's had it rough these past few years," April reminded. "She lost her father *and* sister."

"She won't lose me," Lee declared, and added, "Tomorrow."

"Yes?"

"Let's spend it together; just the three of us."

"What about your hotel?" April asked. "You and Brian have to meet your new partner."

"Hotel can wait," Lee declared, and he glanced down at April. "Is that all right with you?"

April's face flushed with pleasure. She smiled and nodded her acceptance.

Chapter thirteen

Rachel's parents were overjoyed when we announced the good news during breakfast. They not only agreed; they insisted that we live with them.

Rachel looked excited and blissful, and I was happy for her.

After breakfast, Lee, April, and June saddled their horses and rode out. I saddled up too, and then I returned to the main house to tell everyone goodbye.

Afterwards, Rachel walked with me to my horse, and her face was pinched with concern.

"Please be careful," she said.

"Always."

"Last time you left, you didn't show up again for months," she reminded.

"Time flies sometimes," I jested.

"Just remember; we'll be waiting for you."

"We," I repeated, and smiled at the thought.

"Go ahead and kiss me, and then you'd best be off," Rachel said.

So I did.

***

I trotted Desperate to town. He was a tall, smooth traveling sorrel, and was always full of energy.

I broke him several years back for Mr. Tomlin. And, when I left later on a cattle drive, Mr. Tomlin gave him to me for a job well done.

Ol' Desperate was beginning to show his age some. But, he was still my favorite mount, and I rode him most of the time.

I received several curious looks as I rode down the main street. I pulled up at the doctor's office, tied Desperate to the hitching rail, went inside, and asked the doctor to ride out to the Tomlins.

He agreed, and he grabbed his bag and followed me outside.

"How's Ross?" I asked.

"Physically, he'll be fine."

"Glad to hear that," I said.

"I wish I could say the same for his mental health," the doctor added.

"Oh?" I prompted.

The doctor studied me a moment, then said, "Perhaps you should talk to him."

"What's wrong with him?"

"I wish I knew."

"You really think I could help?"

"You just might."

"All right," I decided. "I will."

Chapter fourteen

Ross was at the jail.

I strolled down the main street. As always, my gun hand hovered naturally over my Colt's handle, and I took long, careful strides.

I paused at our old house and looked it over.

My crude paint job was beginning to peel, and the door hung a little crooked. I also noticed a cracked window.

My face was emotionless, but on the inside I was flooded with memories.

As a bachelor, I had lived here with Ross, Lee, and Brian. Then, Rachel and I lived here as newlyweds.

Those had been some happy times. It hadn't been all that long ago, but it sure felt like it.

My memories turned bitter as I remembered what happened next. I was fired as sheriff for not arresting Lee and Brian, and the town council hired Ross the next day.

My dismissal still bothered me, and I reckon I did hold a small grudge. But, I wasn't one to dwell on the past, and I'd moved on. Or had tried to.

I walked on, and I was almost at the jail when I heard running footsteps from behind. Instincts took over, and I palmed my Colt and spun around.

A tall, thin man wearing a business suit stopped abruptly. He took a small step back and held his hands up.

"Don't shoot!" He exclaimed. "It's me, Fred Stilwell!"

I frowned my displeasure. Fred owned the bank, and he was also a member of the town council.

"What do you want, Fred," I said, my voice flat.

"We heard you were in town."

"You heard right."

"We'd like to talk to you," he said.

"We?"

"The city council," he explained.

"What about?" I narrowed my eyes.

"Did you hear what happened to Ross?"

"I did."

"He's going to be out of commission for a while, and we need a replacement as soon as possible. We've had trouble."

"Temporary replacement, or permanent?"

"It depends on who we hire."

A few seconds passed while I thought on that, and I frowned my disapproval.

"You mean if you like him more than Ross," I said.

"I wouldn't put it like that," Fred's face stiffened. "We like Ross. Like him a lot. But, it's obvious he lacks experience."

"You offering me the job?" I asked abruptly.

"We've discussed it."

"You already fired me once," I reminded.

"But that's all been cleared up now," Fred insisted.

I had a bad taste in my mouth, and I didn't say anything.

"The job would also come with the house," Fred reminded.

That was an intriguing thought, and I pinched my face in consideration.

"I'll think on it," I said.

"Of course, Mr. Landon," Fred said. "Take all the time you need."

I nodded. Then I turned, stepped up onto the porch, and walked inside the jail.

Chapter fifteen

Ross was in the living quarters, lying in his bunk. He was on his back, staring at the ceiling. He glanced at me as I walked in, but his face remained emotionless.

His shoulder and hand were bandaged, and I could see red stains where the blood had soaked through.

"Ross," I said.

"You're back."

"We rode in yesterday."

"Rachel?"

"She's fine, and so is April."

Ross nodded and heaved a relieved sigh.

"Glad to hear that."

There was a chair beside his bunk, and I swung my leg over it and sat.

"How you feel?" I asked.

"I forgot how much it hurts to be shot."

"I hear you're lucky to be alive," I said.

"Don't feel lucky."

"But you could be dead," I insisted.

Ross didn't reply, and the silence was awkward. But I didn't say anything; I just waited patiently.

"Walked right into it," Ross finally said, his voice tired and angry. "I was a fool. Got shot in the back, and even lost my thumb."

"Well, I'm glad you aren't feeling sorry for yourself," I said wryly.

"Just stating facts," Ross said matter-of-factly.

"Could have happened to anybody," I insisted.

"But it didn't. It happened to me," Ross replied. "You would have known better."

"We don't know that," I argued. "Every situation is different."

"And you always handle everything perfectly," Ross said, sarcasm in his voice.

I didn't reply as I studied Ross.

"You upset with me?" I finally asked.

"I guess not," Ross sighed. "It's just that you're everything I *want* to be."

I was startled.

"I ain't perfect," I replied. "Just ask Rachel."

Ross didn't even smile, and a few seconds passed.

"How long until you get back on your feet?" I asked, purposely changing the subject.

"Week or so."

I nodded and asked carefully, "Have you talked with the town council lately?"

"No," Ross replied. "But, I need to."

"Oh?" I prompted.

Ross hesitated, but then shrugged.

"You might as well know," he said. "I'm quitting."

"What for?" I raised an eyebrow.

"I ain't qualified," Ross replied. "And, everybody knows it."

"You know more about the law than anybody in this town," I objected.

"Big difference between knowing the law and enforcing it."

"You're decent with a Colt," I said truthfully. "Most the time, that's good enough."

"I'm not as good as you."

"Most aren't."

Ross snorted but didn't reply.

"You won't change your mind?" I asked after a moment.

"Nope."

"They offered me the job," I said suddenly.

If Ross was surprised, he didn't show it. Instead, he looked at me with a blank face.

"And?"

"I wanted to talk to you first."

"Well, now you have."

"If not for recent developments, I wouldn't be interested," I said.

"Oh?"

I told him about the baby. He tried hard not to show it, but I could tell he was envious.

"Congratulations," he said.

"Thanks."

"I always thought I'd make a good father."

"You will, one of these days," I tried to be helpful.

Ross snorted again and looked away.

"So, do you have any objections?" I asked.

"Nope. Take the job if you want."

"I'll need a deputy," I hinted.

"Not a chance," Ross grunted.

"You sure?"

"I'm sure."

I nodded and asked, "What will you do then?"

"No plans. Anyway, nobody cares what I do."

"I care," I declared.

Ross looked at me a moment.

"Well, that makes one," he said.

Chapter sixteen

"I'd best be on my way," I said a few minutes later, and stood.

"Going somewhere?" Ross asked.

I nodded and explained about my trip to Midway to see Tussle.

"You were excited about working for him," Ross recalled.

"Was," I agreed. "But, I have responsibilities to consider."

"I don't," Ross said, and he suddenly looked thoughtful.

"You ain't married," I replied.

Ross didn't seem to hear me.

"Tussle has a big outfit," he commented.

"Does," I agreed.

"You think Tussle would hire me?"

"Probably," I replied. "He's short on help."

"It'd be a fresh start," Ross mused. "Chance to start over."

"I'll mention it to Tussle," I offered.

Ross nodded slowly.

"I'd appreciate that."

"Glad to do it," I said, and then I offered my hand. "You take care now."

Ross shook my hand with his good hand.

"Have a good trip," he said.

"What could go wrong?" I asked wryly.

"With you? Plenty."

I grinned and started for the door.

"Rondo," Ross stopped me.

"Yes?" I paused and looked back.

"They were looking for you."

"Who was?"

"The fellers that shot me."

I narrowed my eyes at that.

"What for?" I asked.

"They didn't say," Ross said, and then he told me what they looked like. "The youngest looked familiar," he finished. "But, I can't place him."

"Well, if they ain't careful, they'll find me," I declared.

Ross smiled for the first time.

"I knew you'd say that," he said.

I grinned at Ross and left.

***

I had just stepped into the saddle when I spotted Fred Stilwell. I kicked up Desperate and rode over to him.

"Be gone a week or two," I told him. "If the sheriff's job still available when I get back, I'll consider it."

Fred looked pleased.

"We can wait that long," he replied. "The job's yours."

I nodded.

"Might paint the house while I'm gone," I suggested. "My wife would appreciate that."

"Of course, Mr. Landon."

"And fix the window and door. I don't want my family catching a cold."

"Anything you say, Mr. Landon," Fred agreed, and asked, "Anything else?"

I thought a moment.

"That'll do for now," I said, and I kicked up Desperate to a brisk trot and left town.

Part Three
"Hotel Business and Little Man"

Chapter seventeen

It had been a long time since I'd traveled anywhere by myself. I enjoyed the ride, and the silence was welcome.

I pointed Desperate north. Then I gave him his head, and he picked his way through the brush at an easy pace.

The country around Empty-lake had occasional mesquite bushes and catclaw, with gentle hills and a few trees scattered about.

There was a cool, pleasant breeze blowing, and we made good time.

It was a good time to think, and I took advantage of it. I recalled my outlaw years, and the lessons learned. I also thought of Yancy and Cooper, Lee and Brian, and even Winchester.

But mostly, I thought of Rachel and the baby.

More than once, I found myself smiling at the thought of a family. And, by evening time, I was even getting excited about it.

I was so deep in thought, I failed to notice when Desperate started limping. And, by the time I did notice, he was really starting to labor.

"What's this?" I asked, surprised.

I dismounted, and concern filled my face as I studied Desperate's front leg.

Already, his tendon was swelling and trembling.

"What'd you do?" I asked out loud.

I ran my hand down his leg, and he flinched in pain and picked his foot up.

"Take it easy, boy," I said, and I straightened up and scowled at my misfortune.

It looked like a strained tendon. That was bad, because recovery time could take months, if at all.

I pinched my face in thought, and then spoke out loud.

"Well, reckon we'll camp here tonight," I told my horse. "We'll figure out what to do in the morning."

Desperate had no objections. While he stood there, I unsaddled him. Then, I gathered some wood, built a fire, and made camp.

Chapter eighteen

After breakfast the next morning, Lee and Brian saddled up and headed towards Empty-lake. They rode side by side in an easy trot.

It was early, and the sun was just coming up. Lee felt good, and he couldn't help but smile.

"Sorry about yesterday," he told Brian.

Brian raised an eyebrow.

"What about it?"

"Spending all day with April and June. I'm sure you're anxious about the hotel."

Brian grunted and waved his hand at Lee.

"You had more important things to take care of."

Lee nodded and grinned.

"How'd yesterday go?" Brian asked after a moment.

"A little awkward at times," Lee admitted, and then he chuckled. "That June; she's really something. Loves to play marbles."

"That's important," Brian remarked.

"What is?"

"Finding things you enjoy doing together."

"Enjoy?" Lee objected. "She beat me eight times."

"Who wins ain't important," Brian frowned.

"Is to me."

"It's spending time with her that counts," Brian pointed out.

"Mebbe so," Lee agreed, but then complained, "Still, she could let me win at least *once*."

Brian grunted and shook his head.

"How are things with April?" He asked.

"No problems there," Lee grinned.

"Have you two discussed marriage?"

"Some."

"And?" Brian prompted.

"We're taking things slow," Lee replied. "No need to rush."

"Just don't wait too long," Brian cautioned. "You mess around a few years, and then some morning you'll wake up and be as old as *I* am."

"I won't wait *that* long."

"Good," Brian declared.

"I just want to make sure everything is running smoothly with the hotel, and that I have something to offer her."

"You expecting trouble?"

"We've never even met our new partner," Lee reminded. "He might not be thrilled to see us."

"I don't care what mood he's in," Brian replied. "It's *our* hotel."

"It is," Lee agreed. "I just hope our new partner knows about it."

"He'll find out soon enough," Brian declared.

"Yes," Lee agreed, "he will."

Chapter nineteen

As I sat around the campfire drinking coffee, I recalled passing a cabin a few miles back.

I figured my best move was to go there. Hopefully, I could borrow a horse and ride back to Empty-lake.

After breakfast the next morning, I threw my saddle on Desperate's back and took out in a walk, leading Desperate behind me.

To my disappointment, Desperate seemed worse. The leg was still swollen, and he limped noticeably with each step.

I don't know why, but by midmorning I got the feeling that I was being watched. I stopped several times and took a long, careful look around. I never saw anything, but I still couldn't shake the feeling.

I reached the cabin just before noon, and I stopped a moment and looked the place over.

The cabin was nestled between two steep hills.

There was a set of pole corrals beside the cabin, and beyond that was a fenced lot. Inside the lot was a dirt tank full of rainwater, and I smiled when I spotted a horse.

Overall, the place was a bit run down, but still nice enough.

"Let's go," I tugged on Desperate's reins.

I spotted cobwebs covering the doorway as I got closer to the cabin, and I figured whoever lived here had been gone for a while.

My suspicions were confirmed when I spotted a note written out on a piece of cowhide, nailed to the front door.

I dropped Desperate's reins and stepped forward.

I had taught Desperate how to ground rein, and he stood still while I cleared away the cobwebs and read the note out loud.

"Gone for a spell. If you're hungry, there's canned goods inside. If you steal something, I'll find you. Depending on what is stolen, I'll either shoot or hang you."

I chuckled at that.

"Sounds like my sort of fellow," I told Desperate, and I opened the door and went inside.

It was a one-room cabin. As expected, everything was dusty, and there were cobwebs hanging from the ceiling. There was a bunk off to the side, a table and a few chairs in the middle, a fireplace, some crudely built shelves, and a small desk in the corner.

My curiosity was kindled as I wondered who lived here. Whoever he was, I hoped he wouldn't mind if I borrowed his horse.

I found a pencil in the desk. I went back outside, and I talked out loud while I wrote a note beneath his on the cowhide.

"My horse is bad crippled, so I'm borrowing yours. I will ride to Empty-lake, and I'll return with your horse and pick up mine. Rondo Landon."

I grunted my satisfaction. I returned the pencil to the desk, shut the door, and looked at Desperate.

"Let's have a look at this horse," I suggested.

Chapter twenty

Lee and Brian received several curious looks as they rode into Empty-lake. They pulled up at the hotel, dismounted, tied their horses to the hitching rail, and stepped up onto the porch.

"Ready?" Lee asked.

Brian nodded, so they pushed through the batwing doors. They paused and allowed their eyes to adjust, and then they took a slow look around.

The hotel was spotless. The mahogany bar gleamed, the glassware shone, and the floor looked polished.

"Home sweet home," Brian said softly.

Lee nodded and asked, "You ever notice how profitable this hotel looks when we're not around?"

"It'll be profitable for us too," Brian declared, and he gestured with his head. "Look. They replaced the mirror."

"Sure did," Lee said, impressed. "Fancy."

Neither Lee nor Brian recognized the bartender. He was looking at them with an expectant smile.

"Help you?" He asked.

"You sure can," Lee drawled as they walked over. "We'd like to see, uh-," he paused and frowned. "Well, whoever's running this place."

"You mean Ed?"

"That'll work."

"I'm afraid he's busy."

"He'll want to see us," Lee declared.

"Why's that?"

"I'm Lee Mattingly, and this here is Brian Clark."

The bartender's eyes widened.

"Heard of you boys," he said.

"Most have," Lee smiled patiently.

"I'll tell Ed you're here."

"You do that."

The bartender hurried around the bar and disappeared in the back. He reappeared a few moments later.

"Ed will see you," he said.

"Figured he would," Lee replied.

"He's in his office. It's underneath the stairs."

Lee grinned at that and said, "Yes, we know."

Chapter twenty-one

I led Desperate over to the pole corrals. I tied him to the
fence, unsaddled him, and pulled my rope off my saddle.
Then, I walked out into the lot where the other horse was.

As soon the horse spotted me, he threw his head up and
snorted.

I couldn't help but sigh my displeasure.

He was the ugliest horse I had ever seen. He was short,
thin, and chicken boned. His color was a mixture of a bay
and roan, with little white dots sprinkled all over his back.

There were also some healed-over spur marks on his
shoulders, and that could only mean one thing.

Trouble.

"Well, Little Man," I named him. "You ain't much to
look at. But, long as I can ride you, I don't reckon it
matters."

Little Man snorted again, shook his head, and took off in
a lope.

I had already built a loop, and I rolled the loop out in
front of him. He stepped into it perfectly, and I jerked the
slack and braced for the impact. But, to my surprise, Little
Man stopped abruptly and just stood there.

He didn't move a muscle as I walked up to him, and I
patted him all over to see how he'd react. But, he was calm,
even when I patted him in the flank.

"Well, you seem gentle enough," I commented.

He backed his ears when I spoke, and I chuckled.

I led him inside the pole corral, shut the gate, and
slipped the bridle on. He took it with no problems, and I
felt a slight sense of hope that those spur marks were a
thing of the past. Perhaps, he was just an easy-going cow
pony now.

Just maybe.

Little Man stood there all gentle-like while I saddled him, and he almost went to sleep on me. He didn't even grunt when I jerked the cinch tight.

I stepped back and studied him. He had his head down, twitching his tail lazily at flies.

On a whim, I grabbed my hat and threw it under his belly.

I was expecting him to at least jump. But instead, Little Man raised his head and looked at me as if I'd gone crazy.

I grabbed my hat, put it back on, and frowned suspiciously.

"You're too gentle," I grumbled.

Again, he backed his ears, but that was all.

Before I climbed on, I unbuckled my gun belt and hung it on the fence.

From experience, I had learned that it was best not to go for a bronc ride with a Colt strapped around your waist. It was just one more thing to get hung up in.

I led Little Man in a circle to loosen him up, but he seemed disinterested.

I stepped up beside him, and with my left hand I held the reins and also the saddle horn.

"You be nice, and I'll be nice," I said, and he backed his ears again.

I watched him a moment. Then I took a little hop, placed my foot in the stirrup, and swung on.

Chapter twenty-two

Lee and Brian walked to the back of the hotel, and they spotted two men underneath the stairs.

One was sitting in a chair; the other was leaning against the wall. The way they were positioned, it was obvious they were guarding the office.

The one sitting had a mouthful of tobacco. His jaw ground slowly, and his lips had a brown tint to them. His Colt revolver hung easy on his hip, and his gun hand hovered naturally over the handle.

He was middle sized, with a leathery face, a hard jaw, and cold eyes. Even if he had wanted to look friendly, it was doubtful he could with that face.

He wasn't trying to look friendly now.

He watched Lee and Brian's every move. His fingers twitched in anticipation, and he continued to chew his tobacco methodically.

His companion was even uglier.

He was slim hipped, and stood at least six feet tall. He had a twisted, killer's face, and there was a mean gleam in his eyes.

He held a tobacco sack in his left hand, and he was in the process of pouring tiny, brown flakes onto a piece of paper. Next, he twirled the cigarette into shape, licked the paper's edges, and sealed them together. Then he struck a match against the wall, lit up, and tossed the match into a nearby spittoon.

He took a deep puff, and only then did he glance at Lee and Brian.

Several seconds passed while they looked at each other.

"We're expected," Lee finally broke the silence.

The man sitting twitched his fingers again. Other than that, neither one did anything.

"Reckon we'll go in now," Lee said, his voice flat.

Neither one replied.

The man sitting leaned over the spittoon and spat out a long, brown stream. He straightened in his chair and looked back at Lee and Brian with the same cold, hard eyes.

They looked at each other some more, and then Lee and Brian moved to the door.

Lee considered knocking, but decided against it. He opened the door abruptly and walked in, and Brian followed him.

Chapter twenty-three

Several seconds passed while I got myself settled in the saddle.

I had a firm grip on the reins, and I grabbed the saddle horn and held on tight with my other hand. I also squeezed my legs up against the swells of my saddle as tight as I could.

I was ready as I'd ever be. I breathed deeply and gently nudged Little Man forward with my spurs.

To my surprise, Little Man had the best handle I had ever seen. He was extremely light, and he could turn on a dime and have five cents left over.

I turned him around a time or two, and then I kicked him up to a trot.

He was the smoothest traveling horse I had ever ridden. It was like rocking in a rocking chair, and we trotted around the pen several times.

"How about that," I said out loud.

As soon as the words were out of my mouth, he exploded like a stick of dynamite.

I've ridden lots of broncs. However, no horse, not even Desperate when he was younger, compared to Little Man.

He had tricks I'd never seen. His jumps were high and twisting. When he landed, he drove his legs into the ground, pounding my insides to pieces.

One jump we were headed towards the New Mexico Territory; the next we headed towards Louisiana. Little Man just couldn't make up his mind.

I lost a stirrup. Then my hat. Then both stirrups.

Little Man took another huge jump. I went flying upwards as he sucked backwards and disappeared beneath me.

I felt like a baby bird trying to fly as I came down. I did a flip in the air and landed with a thud on my back. The violent collision knocked the air from me, and all I could do was gasp like a squealing pig.

A long, desperate minute passed. I could finally inhale, and my face felt hot and flushed while I sucked air into my burning lungs.

Once I recovered somewhat, I checked myself over to be sure nothing was broken. Nothing appeared to be, so I sat up and glared at Little Man.

He was just standing there, his head down, half asleep.

"Little Man," I said. "Either I'm getting soft, or you can really buck."

He backed his ears in response, but I ignored him as I struggled to my feet, grimaced, and walked towards him.

"Probably a little of both," I muttered.

Chapter twenty-four

Lee shut the door to the office and looked around.

A thin, frail man was seated behind the desk. His hands were folded across his chest, and he displayed a smug look.

In the corner, beside the safe, stood two more men. Both had a hard look about them, and Lee felt an instant wariness.

"Come in, gentlemen," the man behind the desk said. "Have a seat."

Lee turned his attention to him.

The first thing he noticed were his upper teeth. They seemed too big for his head, and as a result they stuck over his lower lip.

Lee stared in fascination. They walked over to the desk, but they remained standing. Lee also positioned himself so he could keep an eye on the two in the corner.

"You know who we are," Lee said. "Who might you be?"

"Yes, introductions should be made," he said pleasantly. "My name is Ed Hazel. I'm the owner of the Palace Hotel."

Lee grunted at that.

"And these two?" He gestured.

"I figured you'd know each other," Ed said, surprised.

"Never had the pleasure," Lee shook his head.

"Allow me to introduce you," Ed replied. "This is Curt and Rod Tisdale."

"Heard of you," Lee sounded impressed as he looked at them. "Never met you though."

"Now you have," the shortest one spoke.

"Which one are you?" Lee asked.

"Rod."

Lee nodded and glanced at the other one.

"And you'd be Curt."

"I am," he said, his voice surprisingly deep.

"Well, at least you two talk," Lee commented.

"We like to be friendly," Rod smiled.

"What about the fellers outside the door?" Lee jabbed a thumb in their direction.

"Can't speak for them," Rod said.

Lee grunted, and they looked at each other some more. Several seconds passed, but nobody spoke.

Curt was a large, solid man with straight, heavy features, and he had the marks of a lot of hard, mean years on his face. He wore two Colt revolvers with ivory handles.

Rod only wore one Colt. He had a light, wiry frame, and his eyes were intelligent and calculating.

Rod grinned at Lee, and little character wrinkles formed around the corners of his eyes.

"We've heard of you too," he said. "So, we all know each other."

"Saves time," Lee replied.

"Does," Rod nodded, and said, "You've ridden with Rondo Landon."

"Some."

"Never had a chance to go up against him," Rod said, almost wistfully.

Lee smiled at that.

"You wouldn't be here if you had."

"He's that good?" Rod looked interested.

"He is."

"Better than you?"

"Never been tested."

"Course, you've never seen me and Curt work," Rod pointed out.

"I haven't."

"Maybe you'll get the chance," Rod said, and his eyes twinkled.

"Mebbe so," Lee said.

Everyone was quiet then, waiting for the subject to go to another place.

"You fellers new to town?" Lee finally asked.

"Just rode in yesterday," Rod said.

"Passing through?"

"No, we work for Mr. Hazel."

"That so," Lee said, and asked flatly, "Doing what."

"Whatever Mr. Hazel wants."

Lee looked thoughtful as he looked back at Ed, who seemed fascinated by the conversation.

"How about the fellers at the door? They work for you too?" Lee asked.

"They do," Ed acknowledged.

"Where'd they come from?"

"They didn't say," Ed replied truthfully.

"Seemed like charming fellers," Lee said wryly.

Ed chuckled at that.

"They're a bit dry, but they follow orders."

"And that's good enough for you?" Lee frowned his disapproval.

"It is for now," Ed replied.

"They have names?" Lee wanted to know.

"They call themselves Chewy and Quirley," Ed informed with a grin. "They claim to be cousins."

Lee nodded. He glanced at Brian; then looked back at Ed.

"I didn't realize it took so many gun hands to run a hotel," he said.

"It does in this town," Ed declared.

"How so?"

"We've had trouble recently."

"We heard about that."

"Our sheriff can't seem to handle his responsibilities," Ed continued. "So, I hired these gentlemen to handle any unpleasantness. I want peace and order, and I don't care who we have to kill to get it."

"We?" Lee looked curious.

"Curt, Rod, Chewy, and Quirley," Ed corrected. "But, I'll be with them in spirit."

"I'm sure you will be," Lee said wryly, and asked, "Is this protection for the whole town?"

"I don't own the town; just the hotel."

"I see."

"Ross is a good man," Brian spoke for the first time, and there was displeasure in his voice.

"Clearly not good enough," Ed replied bluntly.

"He was ambushed," Brian defended him. "It could have happened to anybody."

"Perhaps, but it won't happen to Curt, Rod, Chewy, and Quirley," Ed declared.

"I don't imagine it will," Lee agreed, and he glanced once more at Curt and Rod.

"I assume that's why you're here," Ed said.

"How's that?" Lee looked back at him.

"I spread word that I was looking for experienced gun hands."

"Is that so."

"I presume you want a job?" Ed looked at Lee, and then at Brian.

Lee smiled at that and almost chuckled.

"Not hardly," he said.

Chapter twenty-five

I grabbed the reins and led Little Man in another big circle.

It wasn't so much for him. It was more for me, to loosen up and give me a chance to catch my breath.

Little Man seemed bored, and he trailed along behind me like an old, broke cow pony.

But I knew better now.

"Little Man," I said as I walked up beside him. "Like it or not, I'm *going* to ride you back to town. You have no choice in the matter. So you'd best behave yourself and quit this foolishness."

Again, Little Man's response was to back his ears. I sighed, grabbed the saddle horn, and stepped into the saddle.

Like before, he just stood there while I got myself settled. Finally, I said a silent prayer and nudged him forward.

He broke into his smooth trot again, and we went around the corral several times. I was rigid and tense as I expected him to explode at any moment, but he never did.

I stopped him abruptly, spun him around, and kicked him up to a lope.

To my delight, he had the gentlest, cat-like lope I had ever seen. We went around and around, and then I slid him to an abrupt stop.

We stood still a few seconds, and Little Man waited patiently for my next command.

I was confused, and I pinched my face in thought.

Usually, horses didn't stop bucking on their own. Instead, they had to be taught that bucking was frowned upon. And, judging by the spur marks, I figured Little Man hadn't been taught that lesson yet.

I finally decided to make him buck for his own good. The plan was to ride him and teach him a lesson he'd never forget.

Problem was, I couldn't get him to buck.

I tried everything. I popped him in the shoulder with the end of my reins. I kicked him in the flank. I even pulled my rope off my saddle and hung a loop under his tail.

Through it all, he acted like the gentlest kid horse I'd ever come across.

I shook my head in wonder while I coiled my rope.

"I can't figure you out," I said out loud.

His head shot up abruptly as soon as I said that, and he exploded. He went straight up into the air, and the sudden movement snapped my head like a whip.

He bucked so hard, it felt like I shrunk a foot each time we hit the ground.

I almost bit my tongue off on the third jump. Then he sucked backwards, and I went flying through the air. I hit the top rail, bounced, and landed in a heap on the other side of the corrals.

The dust settled slowly, and after a moment I groaned and rolled over.

I came face to face with Little Man. He was just standing there, twitching his tail lazily, looking at me through the rails of the corral.

I wondered briefly if I should just walk back to town.

Chapter twenty-six

"If not a job, then why *are* you here?" Ed asked.

Lee glanced at Brian; then looked back at Ed.

"Not sure how to answer that," he admitted.

"How about at the beginning?" Ed suggested, and added, "And *please*; have a seat. Make yourselves comfortable."

They sat.

Then Lee said, "Brian and I built this hotel."

"You did a fantastic job," Ed acknowledged.

"Thanks," Lee said, and continued, "We also had a silent partner named Jessica."

"A woman?" Ed raised an eyebrow.

"She had money; we didn't," Lee explained.

"I see."

"Then we ran into some financial problems," Brian spoke up.

"We sure did," Lee said, and his face darkened with the painful memory.

"That's when Jeremiah became a partner," Brian said.

"And now, Jeremiah is dead," Lee added.

"I was sad to hear about that," Ed said. "I liked him."

It was obvious Ed was lying, but Lee and Brian managed to nod.

"I believe I know the rest of the history lesson," Ed continued. "Ike Nash acquired your share of the hotel. After Ike's unfortunate death, Jeremiah became the full owner. Then I became a partner, and now I'm the owner."

Lee smiled wryly and said, "Not quite."

"How so?" Ed frowned.

"We got Jessica's share back after we killed – I mean – Ike was killed," Lee said.

"How did you accomplish that?" Ed asked, startled.

Neither Lee nor Brian replied, and several seconds passed.

Ed looked thoughtful. He cleared his throat and asked, "Jeremiah and Jessica were partners?"

"For a short while," Brian said.

"A *very* short while," Lee said.

"What happened?" Ed asked.

"We sort of acquired Jessica's share," Lee explained.

Ed nodded slowly, and a heavy silence filled the room. A long minute passed. Then Ed laughed, but not humorously.

"Are you suggesting that you're my partners?"

"Not suggesting," Lee corrected. *"Telling."*

"That's quite a story."

"Glad you liked it," Lee said.

"I assume you have proof?"

"Proof?" Lee frowned.

"Legal documentation of any kind?"

Lee gave Brian a questioning look.

Brian frowned in thought. Then he sighed and shook his head.

"No proof," he said softly.

Ed looked relieved. He smiled, and his teeth showed even more.

This time, Lee didn't find it so fascinating.

Chapter twenty-seven

I led Little Man in another circle, and he followed obediently like a good little horse.

I limped up beside him. I started to climb on, but then I paused.

We looked at each other, and the only sound was my heavy breathing.

"Little Man," I said. "I can't figure you out."

Like before, he backed his ears as soon as I spoke.

A thought suddenly occurred to me. It was a bizarre notion, but the more I thought on it, the more sense it made.

"Little Man," I said again, and he backed his ears.

I took a small step back, and we looked at each other some more.

Then I said, "Hey!"

As soon as I spoke, he backed his ears.

"You don't like the sound of my voice," I said. "Is that it?"

He backed his ears in response.

I scratched my jaw in thought. Then, I stepped into the saddle and kicked him up to a trot.

Round and round we went. Then we loped. Then I spun him around. Then backed him up. Then we trotted some more.

I rode him around that corral for half an hour, and we did every maneuver imaginable. I never said a word, and he never offered to buck.

I finally pulled him up.

Little Man was lathered with sweat. His sides heaved, and he stood perfectly still.

I almost laughed, but I stopped myself just in time. I wasn't sure if Little Man tolerated laughter or not.

I stepped off him.

Then I said, "Little Man, I've got you figured out."

Little Man backed his ears, and I grinned.

I decided to unsaddle him. I turned toward the gate, and I jumped abruptly in surprise.

There were two men a-horseback beside the cabin, and they were watching me with somber expressions.

One was older than the other.

The older one held a doubled barreled shotgun over his saddle. The hammers were pulled back, and both barrels were pointed at me.

Chapter twenty-eight

"Let's understand my side of this," Ed said.

"Yes, let's," Lee said.

"You have no proof. Yet, you claim to be my partners."

"That is correct."

"You expect me to just step aside and let you take over?"

"That'd be helpful," Lee said.

Ed snorted his disgust.

"I worked hard for this," he replied. "I've a lot invested."

"So do we," Lee said.

"But you lost it all," Ed reminded.

"Did," Lee admitted. "But, we got it back."

"So you say."

Lee leaned forward in his chair and thrust out his jaw.

"You don't believe us."

"I'm sorry, but I don't."

"If we had proof?" Brian spoke up.

"Then I would listen," Ed said, and he chuckled gruffly. "Don't you realize, without proof, *anybody* could march in here and declare themselves a partner?"

"We're not anybody," Lee said.

"You aren't," Ed agreed. "And, because I respect you, I'm going to keep this ridiculous claim of yours quiet."

Lee looked as if he'd just been slapped. He narrowed his eyes as he looked at Ed.

"Ridiculous," he repeated.

"That's how I would describe it," Ed said. "And, any court of law would side with me."

Lee flinched his jaw. Nobody spoke, and the silence was tense.

Ed finally spoke.

"Gentlemen, I have enjoyed our conversation immensely. But, as you might remember, running a hotel takes a lot of work. So if you'll excuse me…"

Neither Lee nor Brian made a move to leave. They just sat there, staring at Ed with emotionless faces.

"What about the hotel," Lee said, his voice flat.

"What about it?"

"We haven't decided anything."

"There's nothing *to* decide," Ed replied. "I own it; you don't."

"You won't change your mind," Lee said, and it sounded more like a statement than a question.

"Not without proof."

"I had hoped you would listen to reason."

"And I have," Ed replied, his voice calm. Then he said, "Gentlemen, we are done here."

"No, we're not," Lee replied.

Ed ignored Lee's comment as he looked at Curt and Rod.

"Will you see these gentlemen out please?"

The Tisdale brothers nodded. With their gun hands hovering nonchalantly over their revolvers, they walked across the room.

"You heard him," Rod said.

Lee and Brian glanced at each other. Brian shook his head slightly, and Lee frowned. They stood, and tension built as they looked at Curt and Rod.

The Tisdale brothers didn't say anything. They just waited.

"We'll go," Lee finally said, his voice soft.

Rod grinned at him.

"Wise decision."

"But we'll be seeing you boys again, *real* soon."

"Looking forward to it," Rod replied.

Brian turned and walked toward the door, but Lee wasn't quite through yet. He continued to look at Rod, and Rod grinned back.

Several seconds passed, and then Lee looked at Curt. It was an intense look, but Curt's face was emotionless as he stared back.

"You don't talk much," Lee said to Curt.

"I do most the talking for both of us," Rod spoke up.

"Interesting," Lee said.

Then Lee turned and followed Brian out.

Chapter twenty-nine

My gun belt hung on the fence beside the gate. Acting unconcerned, I started to lead Little Man over towards it.

The older man saw what I was attempting, and he raised his shotgun.

"You take one more step toward that Colt, and I'll blast you from here to Mexico," he said.

His voice was surprisingly gentle. However, there was something in his tone that told me he wasn't bluffing.

"I won't," I said.

He nodded. Nobody spoke, and several seconds passed while we looked at each other.

The younger one displayed an arrogant smirk, but the older one studied me with a professional wariness. It was a look I knew all too well, and I swallowed uneasily.

I had never seen the older one. However, like Ross, the younger one looked familiar, but I couldn't place him.

"Who are you?" The older one broke the silence.

"Rondo Landon," I said.

He grunted at that. I saw a hint of admiration in his eyes, but there was also some hostility.

"Heard of you."

"Most have."

"You as good with a Colt as they say?"

"Pretty much."

"Fastest gun around, eh?"

"I wouldn't put it like that."

"I heard you betrayed your gang and went honest."

"Not exactly how it happened," I frowned. "But, I am honest."

He gestured at Little Man.

"If you're so trustworthy, why are you stealing that horse?"

"I'm not," I replied, and I gestured at the cabin. "I wrote a note, explaining everything."

"How 'bout explaining it again."

I hesitated, but then I told him what happened. His face was emotionless while he listened.

"Sounds reasonable," he said after I finished.

I breathed a sigh of relief. However, he didn't lower the shotgun or ease the hammers down, and that worried me.

"You don't believe me?" I asked.

"Sure."

"Then why don't you ease those hammers back down," I suggested.

He chuckled gruffly.

"Making you nervous?"

"Just a bit," I admitted.

"I haven't told you who I am yet."

"Oh?"

"For three, long years I've yearned for this moment, meeting you face to face."

"Glad I could help."

He seemed to be enjoying this confrontation, but he was the only one.

"My name's Gage," he announced. "Gage Palmer."

The name meant nothing to me.

"Nice to meet you," I said.

He didn't reply, and he watched me closely.

Several tense seconds passed.

A thought suddenly occurred to me, and I felt a jolt of surprise. I looked into his eyes, and he smiled smugly.

"Did you say *Palmer*?" I asked.

"I did."

"Any relation to a Ryan Palmer?"

He nodded slightly.

"He was my son."

We were quiet as we thought on that.

"Oh, boy," I finally murmured.

"And you killed him," he said, and there was anger in his voice.

Chapter thirty

Lee and Brian sat at a corner table in the only café in town, eating lunch.

The café was a long, narrow room. It wasn't much, but the food was good, and that's all that mattered.

Lee looked sullen and somber.

From experience, Brian knew to give Lee some time to digest what had just happened. They ate their salt pork and beans in silence, and they washed it down with plenty of coffee.

"Well, that didn't go over so good," Brian finally commented.

"When we do something foolish, we go all the way," Lee grumbled.

"We sure do."

"I just realized something," Lee said with a mulish face.

"What's that?"

"I'm a failure."

"Aw, don't be so hard on yourself."

"I failed at being an outlaw. I failed in business. Failed with friendships. Failed in love. You name it," Lee pointed at himself. "I've failed at it."

"We *did* bust out of Huntsville," Brian reminded. "Not many have done that."

Lee thought on that, and shook his head.

"We ended up on a blind horse, wearing filthy clothes with more holes than pockets," Lee argued. "Then, we got shot full of *more* holes a few days later. I wouldn't exactly call that a success story."

"What about April and June," Brian replied. "Things are going good there."

"Just give me time. I'll mess that up too."

Brian looked at Lee a moment. Then he sighed and shook his head.

"I'm just tired of failing all the time," Lee muttered. "It's all I do."

"I wouldn't call ourselves failures *just* yet," Brian replied.

"You heard Ed," Lee argued as he took a swig of coffee. "We have no proof."

"Actually, we just might."

Lee was startled, and he choked on his coffee. He coughed violently and sprayed Brian with a warm mist.

"What?" He managed to say.

Brian scowled his disgust. He pulled out a handkerchief and wiped his face.

"Think back to when Jeremiah became a partner," Brian said as he returned his handkerchief to his pocket.

"His four aces beat my full house," Lee said glumly. "See? More failure."

"*After* that," Brian frowned, and reminded, "I wrote up a contract, declaring Jeremiah a partner. We all signed it."

"And we lost the hotel before the ink dried," Lee replied. "Even *more* failure."

"Since then, the hotel has changed ownership so fast, I doubt anybody took the time to write up new contracts," Brian said as he ignored Lee's comment. "They were probably all verbal agreements."

"What are you implying?" Lee narrowed his eyes.

"I'm suggesting," Brian replied, "that it is *just* possible that the last signed contract states you, me, and Jeremiah as partners."

Lee scratched his jaw in thought.

"What about all the other ownership changes since then?" He asked.

"Hard to prove a handshake."

"I see your point," Lee nodded slowly, and asked, "Where is this contract?"

"I put our copy in the safe."

Lee looked startled.

"The safe in the hotel?"

"Yep."

"Why didn't you say something awhile ago?"

Brian shot Lee a dark look.

"You think Ed would've opened up the safe and let us look?"

"Probably not," Lee admitted.

"Then that's why."

"He might've already gotten rid of the contract," Lee reasoned. "If'n I was him, I'd have burned it."

"Or, he might not know about it," Brian argued. "The file I put that contract in had a lot of building receipts and whatnot. It's possible he overlooked it."

Lee looked thoughtful, and he smiled after a moment.

"You realize, there's only one way to find out."

"I realize."

"You willing to go that far?"

"If you are."

"Perhaps we should talk to Ross first," Lee suggested. "See if he can do something."

"Couldn't hurt," Brian agreed.

"If there's a way to go about it legal, Ross would know."

"And if there's not?" Brian asked.

"Then we'll do things *our* way."

"You mean not legal."

"More or less," Lee grinned.

"Just like old times," Brian drawled.

"Except we'll be robbing our own hotel," Lee pointed out.

"Yes, except for that."

Chapter thirty-one

Gage's face was twisted with the painful memory of losing his son. Then his remorse turned to anger, and his trigger finger twitched anxiously.

I expected to be shot at any moment. However, instead of fear, a cold, killing feeling grabbed ahold of me.

This feeling ran in our family. Yancy and Cooper have felt it, as have others.

It's a feeling that's hard to explain. Best way is to say that it's a feeling of confidence, calmness, loneliness, sharp keenness, and pure meanness all rolled up into one.

Nobody has been able to explain this feeling; it just shows up in times of distress. And, whenever any Landon gets this feeling, whoever stirred it up was in trouble.

My thoughts turned to survival. Someway, somehow, I *had* to survive. I just had too much to live for.

I eyed my six-shooter hanging on the fence, and I wondered briefly about making a dive for it.

As if he were reading my thoughts, Gage said to his son, "Clint, get his gun belt."

I tried to hide my disappointment as he rode over to the corral. With an arrogant smirk, Clint pulled my Colt out of the holster and examined it.

Now that I knew who he was, it was remarkable how much Clint looked like his brother. He had the same build with the same curly, blond hair. He also displayed the same foolish smirk on his face, and seeing it brought back a flood of unpleasant memories.

"Pa, we just captured the great Rondo Landon without firing a shot," he drawled.

"That is correct, son."

I frowned. Even Clint's voice sounded like Ryan Palmer.

Clint looked at me, and his face filled with scorn.

"We could've shot you anytime we wanted," he bragged. "You never even saw us."

"I was busy," I replied.

"Soon as we spotted you, we figured you were Rondo. You fit the description, and you also had *this*," he said as he held up my ivory handled Colt.

"Congratulations."

"I don't see any notches in the handle," he said, and he motioned at his own Colt. "I've got six notches in mine."

"If I did that cheap trick, I wouldn't have much of a handle left," I replied.

Anger flashed across his face, but then he grinned as the confidence returned.

"You won't be so cocky after we're through with you," he snarled. "You killed my brother, and you're going to pay for that."

"It was self defense," I looked at Gage, hoping to see any sign of reasoning.

There was none.

"I don't care how fair it was," Gage spoke up. "All I know is my son is dead."

"He was foolish," I said truthfully.

"That doesn't change anything," Gage said, and I frowned my displeasure.

"So now what?" I demanded.

"I always figured on killing you right off," Gage replied. "But, because of recent developments, I have need of a man with your skills."

I felt a small sense of hope.

"Skills?" I asked.

A pained expression crossed Gage's face as he explained.

"Back in town, Clint lost big at poker a few nights ago. We had to leave in a hurry, and I didn't realize until later that he lost almost everything we've saved these past few years."

"He was cheating!" Clint said, irritation in his voice.

"I'm too old to start over," Gage continued. "I want my money back, and you're going to help."

"How?" I asked carefully.

"We're going to rob the hotel," Gage informed. "And, *you're* going to show us how to do it."

I scowled and shook my head.

"Can't help you," I said.

"You've robbed before."

"Have," I agreed. "But not anymore."

Gage scowled at me.

"If you ain't useful," he warned, and he raised his shotgun a few inches, "there's no use keeping you around."

I eyed the shotgun, and several seconds passed.

"Well?" Gage asked.

I swallowed hard.

"I could always reconsider," I said.

Chapter thirty-two

"Before we go any further, there's something you should think about," Brian said.

"What's that," Lee replied as he took a swig of coffee.

"April and June."

Lee looked at Brian.

"What about them?"

Brian said, "Things go wrong, we could end up on the wrong side of the law again."

"So?"

"You sure you want to take that risk? Might end up losing April and June."

Lee pinched his face in thought but remained silent.

"We could start over someplace else," Brian suggested.

"With what?" Lee snorted. "We're broke."

"We could always find a ranch job."

Lee considered that and shook his head.

"June and April deserve better," he said softly.

"Don't you think that's for them to decide?"

"Perhaps," Lee admitted.

"You could ask April?"

"No," Lee said. "Can't do that."

Brian studied Lee a moment.

Then he said, "All right then."

Lee nodded emphatically, and they drank their coffee in silence. Several minutes passed, but neither one spoke.

"What if Ed changed the combination to the safe?" Lee asked after awhile.

"It's possible, but doubtful."

"How so?"

"We had that safe custom built in Dallas," Brian reminded. "They're the only ones that can change the combination, and that'd be costly."

"I didn't know that."

"Now you do."

Lee grunted, and asked, "Any ideas how we go about this?"

"I'd say carefully," Brian said. "Chewy and Quirley seemed like a handful."

"Don't forget about Curt and Rod."

"Yes, they have quite the reputation," Brian agreed.

"They do," Lee nodded. "And, seeing how they're still alive, they must be good at what they do."

"The Window Brothers," Brian said suddenly.

"What?" Lee looked at him.

"Curt 'n Rod," Brian explained. "Get it? The Window Brothers."

Lee sighed and shook his head.

"Very clever."

"We could call the other fellers the Tobacco Cousins," Brian continued.

"It fits," Lee admitted.

Brian grinned, proud of himself, and Lee sighed again.

"If you put as much thought into robbing that hotel, we'd have a plan already," Lee scolded.

Brian started to chuckle, but his face stiffened before he could.

"Speaking of the Window Brothers; they just walked in," he said quietly.

Lee turned in his chair and spotted them.

They were standing just inside the door, looking the place over. Rod's gaze settled on Lee, and neither one looked away.

"So they have," Lee said softly.

Chapter thirty-three

"I figured you'd change your mind," Gage grunted, and he lowered the shotgun a few inches.

"It's a foolish notion," I tried to reason with him. "Our chances of success would be slim at best."

"If'n I was you, I wouldn't attempt to talk me out of it," Gage replied.

"Why not?"

"Robbing that hotel is the only thing keeping you alive."

I frowned at that, and Gage chuckled gruffly.

"Figured that would keep you quiet," he said.

"Things like this take careful planning," I tried another angle. "Sometimes, it took Kinrich months to plan a job."

"It won't take you that long."

"I'm not so sure," I replied. "A lot of precise preparation goes into each job."

Gage looked at me a moment.

Then he said, "You have tonight."

"What?" I was startled.

"We'll rob the hotel first thing in the morning," Gage decided.

"Why the hurry?"

"It's already been a week."

"A few more days won't matter," I argued.

"Probably wouldn't," Gage agreed. "But, we'll still do it in the morning."

I sighed and let it go.

"What happens after that?" I asked.

"We'll see," Gage said, and he looked at Clint. "Tie him up and get him on his horse. We'd best be going."

Clint nodded. He dismounted, stashed my gun belt in his saddlebags, and pulled some rope out.

"Where we headed?" I asked as Clint opened the gate and walked toward me.

"South," Gage replied.

"Can you be a little more specific?" I asked.

Gage frowned at me.

"We'll head south," he said. "Then west."

I scowled, but Clint reached me before I could reply.

"Turn around, and put your hands behind your back," he instructed.

I didn't move. A sneer crossed Clint's face, and his hand hovered over his gun handle.

"I won't ask again," he warned.

I had no choice but to oblige him. I heaved an inward sigh and turned.

Chapter thirty-four

The table next to Lee and Brian was empty.

Walking slowly and deliberately, Curt and Rod crossed the room and sat.

Lee was impressed as he studied them.

Their every move displayed confidence. Their demeanor was calm and collected, and they seemed to comprehend things easily. Nothing bothered or upset them.

They nodded politely, and Lee and Brian returned the nods.

A waiter came over.

While they ordered, Lee pulled out a cigar. He bit off the end, struck a match, and lit up.

The waiter left. Nobody said anything, and the silence was loud.

Lee took in a deep puff and exhaled. He watched the smoke disappear while he gathered his thoughts.

"Figured you boys would get your meals at the hotel," he finally said.

"Usually do," Rod spoke up.

"This a special occasion?"

Rod's eyes twinkled.

"Not especially. Ed told us to keep an eye on you."

"That so," Lee said.

"Yep."

"He worried about us?"

"Just a touch."

"Well, least we accomplished *something*," Lee grunted, and asked, "You two worried?"

"About you two?"

"Yes."

Rod's smile turned into a grin.

"Not so much."

"Afraid of that," Lee said.

"Understand; we got nothing against you boys," Rod said. "But, business is business."

"And you work for Ed," Lee said.

"That is correct."

It fell silent while Lee thought on that. A few minutes passed, and the waiter brought their food.

"You boys going to walk away from the hotel?" Rod asked between bites.

Lee took a puff on his cigar before he replied.

"Still pondering that."

"Be a mistake if you didn't."

"That a warning?"

"Nope. Just a little free advice."

"Free advice," Lee repeated, and smiled. "I learned a long time ago you usually get what you pay for."

Rod chuckled at that and took a swig of coffee.

"If we had proof, would that change your mind?" Brian spoke up.

Rod smiled patiently.

"We work for Ed."

"What if we paid you more?" Lee slipped in.

"We work for Ed," Rod repeated.

"Loyal," Lee observed.

"Folks in our line of work can't afford a bad reputation," Rod replied.

"I respect that," Lee nodded. "Feel the same way myself."

"Like I said; it's nothing personal."

"Is to us," Lee objected. "It's *our* hotel."

"So you say," Rod smiled.

Lee frowned, and it was silent for the rest of their meal.

Like everything else they did, they ate slow and vigilant. Meanwhile, Lee smoked his cigar and watched them.

When they finished, they placed their utensils in their plates, wiped their mouths, and stood.

"Nice talking to you boys," Rod said.

"A real pleasure," Lee said wryly.

"Plan on being in town long?"

"Thought we'd visit some with the sheriff, if that's all right," Lee said, a bit sarcastic.

"Fine by us," Rod shrugged. "Ed's only instructions were to watch you."

"For now."

"For now," Rod smiled and nodded.

Lee returned the smile and stood, as did Brian.

"Well, nice to know where we all stand," he said.

"It is," Rod agreed.

Lee nodded. He and Brian left the café, and they headed towards the sheriff's office.

Curt and Rod walked out a few moments later. They took a slow, careful look around, and then they strolled down the sidewalk, going in the same direction.

Chapter thirty-five

To my displeasure and discomfort, I discovered that Clint knew what he was doing.

He skillfully tied my hands behind my back, and the knots were tight and harsh. My fingers started going numb after only a few seconds, and my wrists throbbed.

Clint gave me an unexpected shove in the back. I stumbled forward but managed to stay on my feet.

"Get on your horse," he snarled.

"You expect me to ride him like this?" I protested. "You saw him bucking."

"Don't worry; we'll catch him if you fall off."

It was obvious he wasn't concerned about my health, so I said no more as I walked over to Little Man. He was just standing there in the middle of the corral, half asleep.

"Allow me one favor," I looked over at Gage.

"What's that?" Gage looked interested.

I nodded at Desperate, who was still tied to the fence.

"Turn him loose in the lot. At least he'll have water and can graze."

"Looks like he's done for," Gage studied him.

"He'll get over it," I said.

Gage scratched his jaw in thought, and then shrugged.

"I don't have any grudges against the horse," he said.

He dismounted and walked toward Desperate. Meanwhile, I felt a sharp jab in the ribs.

"Get on your horse," Clint said.

I nodded, and with great difficulty I managed to get my foot in the stirrup. Clint had to push on my back to help me up, and there was nothing gentle in the way he went about it.

Meanwhile, Gage untied Desperate, led him over to the lot, opened the gate, and turned him loose.

"Satisfied?" Gage looked at me.

I didn't dare talk on Little Man, so I just nodded.

"Let's go then," he said.

They stepped into their saddles, and Gage led out in a brisk trot. Clint followed, and he led Little Man behind him, taking me along whether I liked it or not.

Chapter thirty-six

Brian knocked on the door to the sheriff's office.

There was no answer, so Lee tried the door. It was unlocked, and they walked in.

The first thing Lee noticed was Ross's gun belt. It hung in clear display on the corner of the desk, and Lee found this amusing.

"Good thing we don't have evil intentions," he gestured at the gun belt, and Brian nodded.

They found Ross in the next room. He was sitting up in his bunk, and his face was pale.

"Ross," Lee said, announcing their arrival.

"Lee," Ross replied, and he nodded at Brian.

Lee and Brian walked over, and several seconds passed as they studied Ross.

"You look horrible," Lee finally said.

"Thanks."

"How do you feel?" Brian spoke up, and he shot Lee a dark look.

"Pretty much how I look."

"You'll feel better," Brian tried to be helpful.

"Perhaps," Ross said. Then, as if he remembered he was sheriff, asked, "You boys need something?"

"We sure do," Lee replied.

Taking turns, they explained what happened. Ross listened, but they could tell he was only partly interested.

"Why tell me all this?" Ross asked when they had finished.

Lee scowled.

"Because you're the sheriff," he said.

"And what do you expect me to do?"

"We figured you could help," Lee replied. "We'd like to be legal about this if we can."

"And if you can't?"

Neither Lee nor Brian replied, and Ross sighed.

"I'm just a small town sheriff," he told them. "What you need is a lawyer."

"For what?" Lee asked.

"To go to trial."

Lee looked thoughtful.

"Hadn't thought of that," he admitted.

"It's how most folks handle their differences," Ross said wryly.

"I'm willing to try new things," Lee replied, and asked, "How long would this trial thingy take?"

"Depends. Could take months."

"Months?" Lee frowned his displeasure.

"Takes time for lawyers to build a case and gather evidence," Ross explained.

"We don't have months," Lee objected.

"I'm not sure you have a choice."

Lee smiled at that.

"We have choices," he said. "And, it wouldn't take months."

"I can imagine."

"You ain't gonna try and talk us out of it?" Lee asked, surprised.

"None of my business," Ross shrugged.

"But you're the sheriff," Lee reminded.

"I won't be for long."

"Oh?" Lee raised an eyebrow, then asked, "What's the matter with you?"

"A lot."

"I can see that," Lee grumbled. He glanced at Brian, then said, "Well, we'd best be on our way."

"Good luck."

"Thanks."

Ross just sat there, staring at the floor, as they turned and left the sheriff's office. They walked down the street to their horses, untied them, and stepped into their saddles.

As they rode out, Curt and Rod watched from the porch of the hotel.

Chapter thirty-seven

To my relief, we traveled in silence.

Little Man trotted along behind Clint like a seasoned packhorse. I never said a word, and he never offered to buck.

I was actually glad to be riding him. It was hard to find any rhythm with my hands tied behind my back. However, smooth as Little Man was, it didn't matter so much.

The afternoon passed slowly. We went south a ways, and then we turned west, just like Gage said.

There was a creek about a mile north of Empty-lake, and we rode up to it late afternoon.

"Be a good place to stop," Gage said, and Clint nodded his agreement.

"Take care of him," Gage gestured at me. "Then gather some firewood."

Clint nodded, stepped off his horse, and walked over to me. He motioned me down, and I carefully stepped off Little Man.

"Get over there and sit down," Clint snarled, and he pointed at a nearby tree.

My hands were so numb I couldn't even feel them, and my shoulders and wrists throbbed. But, I didn't say anything as I did what he said.

I tried to move my fingers, but it was no use. Try as I might, I just couldn't get any blood flowing.

They set up camp while I suffered in silence.

Clint built a fire and cooked supper. Meanwhile, Gage unsaddled and picketed the horses.

He unsaddled Little Man last, and he looked amused as he joined us at the fire.

"That's one ugly horse," he commented.

I couldn't argue with that, so I didn't reply.

Coffee was ready soon. Gage poured a cup and then glanced at me.

"Come up with a plan yet?"

"I could think better without this," I replied, and I lifted my hands.

"Uncomfortable?" Gage asked.

"Just a touch."

Gage thought on that, and then looked at Clint.

"Cut him loose."

"You sure?" Clint objected.

"He's gotta eat, unless you want to feed him."

That was an unpleasant thought for both of us, and Clint said no more. He moved behind me, pulled out his knife, and slashed my bonds.

I immediately started rubbing my wrists. My fingers pulsed as blood returned, and it was a painful process.

Clint snorted his pleasure when he saw me in pain, but I ignored him as I continued to rub.

"Better?" Gage asked after a moment.

"Somewhat," I said. Then I added, "Coffee smells good."

"Help yourself."

I nodded, grabbed the pot, and filled a cup. I took a swig, and then sighed as I felt the warmth trickle down my throat.

"Good coffee," I said.

"Glad you like it," Gage said, then added, "So, tell me what you're thinking."

From the tone of his voice, I could tell his patience was wearing thin. I took another swig of coffee, collected my thoughts, and shared my knowledge.

"There's one thing I learned about the outlaw business early on," I recalled.

"What's that?" Gage asked.

"The best way to rob somebody is with a distraction," I declared.

"How so?" Gage looked interested.

"Nobody can be in two places at once," I replied. "Kinrich always created a disruption at one end of town. Then, while everybody was going one way, Kinrich would ride in from the other direction."

"What sort of disruption?"

"It varied," I said. "Fistfights, gunfights, explosions – all Kinrich needed was a minute or two."

"That might actually work," Gage looked thoughtful.

"Glad you like it," I said. Then I added, "Now we need to figure out a distraction. Bigger the better."

"Already figured one out," Gage said, and smiled wolfishly.

"That was quick," I said, surprised. "What's the distraction?"

"You."

I didn't like how he said that, and I frowned suspiciously.

Chapter thirty-eight

Lee and Brian rode towards Tomlin's headquarters.

Their horses traveled in an easy trot, and they couldn't help but nip at the occasional green clump of grass.

"Eventful day," Brian broke the silence.

"I'll say," Lee agreed.

"I don't think Ross will be any help."

"He doesn't even care," Lee said sourly.

"Didn't seem like."

"He sure has changed," Lee declared.

"I'd say so."

"He and Rondo were always close, but I've never completely trusted Ross," Lee continued. "I always get the feeling that he thinks he's better than us."

"We *are* ex-outlaws," Brian reminded.

"We are," Lee admitted. "But, we aren't the fool who fell head over heels for that no good Lucy Nash."

"She was a beautiful woman," Brian defended him. "It could have happened to anybody."

"But now look at him," Lee objected.

"He's just depressed over getting shot."

"We've been shot plenty of times," Lee argued. "We never got depressed about it."

"That's because we have more experience."

"*That* we do."

"Ross will be fine; he just needs some time," Brian reasoned. "Besides, might be best if he stays out of it. Could get himself killed."

"Might," Lee agreed, and his face turned wistful.

Brian glanced at Lee and noticed his expression.

"What is it?" He prompted.

"The Window Brothers, as you call them."

"What about them?"

Lee hesitated, then said, "I like them."

"You *like* them?" Brian made a face.

Lee nodded.

"Mind explaining that a little?" Brian asked.

"They're honest, straight forward, and good at what they do," Lee pointed out. "In a way, they remind me of us. Only younger."

"They also work for the man who stole our hotel," Brian reminded.

"I know that."

"If Ed wants us dead, they'll probably be the ones coming for us. Them, or the Tobacco Cousins."

"Probably will," Lee agreed, and added wistfully, "I wish there was another way."

"We already tried."

Lee nodded, and it was quiet a moment. But Brian was worried and couldn't let it go.

"If they come for us, we'll have to be alert," he warned.

"Sure will."

"You hesitate, it could be the end for both of us."

Lee looked at Brian a moment.

Then he said, "I won't."

"Just making sure."

Lee didn't reply, and they said no more as they trotted on.

Chapter thirty-nine

To my surprise, Clint was a decent cook. We had salted pork with biscuits, and we washed it down with plenty of coffee.

Clint kept looking at me. He displayed an arrogant smirk, just like his brother had done years ago.

I tried my best to ignore him as I chewed my food, took a swig of coffee, and looked at Gage.

"Perhaps we should discuss this distraction tactic some more," I said.

"No need," Gage replied.

"*I'm* the expert here," I tried again. "You should tell me what you have in mind. It might not work."

"I'll take my chances."

It was obvious he wasn't going to tell me. I sighed and let it go.

I felt Clint's eyes on me. I glanced at him, and he was sneering at me again.

"Enjoying yourself?" I asked.

"As a matter of fact, I am."

"I'm glad somebody is."

Clint was itching to talk. Another minute passed, and he finally just couldn't help himself.

"There's all sorts of stories about you," he declared.

"Reckon there is," I admitted.

"I've heard them all too."

"Congratulations."

"When I was younger, I really wanted to meet you."

"Well, the wait's over."

"I always thought we might be friends."

I didn't want to disappoint him, so I didn't reply. Instead, I asked a question.

"Who told you the stories?"

"My brother," Clint replied, and declared, "You and Ryan were real close before you betrayed him."

"We were?" I raised an eyebrow.

"There's no use denying it," Clint said, and added, "Ryan was always bragging on you."

I pinched my face in thought, and understanding began to dawn on me after a moment.

Ryan had always been jealous of me and wanted my reputation. And, as close as he could get to that was to announce that he and I were friends. That is, until he could kill me and *take* my reputation.

Clint interrupted my thoughts.

"But then, Ryan said you changed."

"It happens," I said.

"You were the most feared outlaw in Texas," Clint said, and his face glowed at the thought. "You, along with Ben Kinrich, Lee Mattingly, and my brother, were unstoppable."

"That's a matter of opinion."

"But then you betrayed your friends. And, not only did you go honest, you also became a sheriff."

"What was I thinking," I said wryly.

"What changed you?"

"My wife had a lot to do with it," I said truthfully.

"You're married?"

"Shocking, I know."

"Why'd you kill my brother?" Clint demanded.

I pondered how to answer that.

It was obvious they didn't know the truth. Problem was, the truth only made Ryan look worse. However, I wasn't one to lie. I took a deep breath and cleared my throat.

"Ryan hated me from the beginning," I declared. "I was everything Ryan *wanted* to be. I could shoot better, and I also rode everywhere with Kinrich. Over the years, Ryan tried to kill me several times. I warned him to leave me alone, but he just wouldn't listen. So, I finally killed him."

Clint narrowed his eyes, and his jaw muscles rippled. He glanced at Gage, who was also glaring at me.

"You're a liar," Gage spoke, his voice low and soft.

"Truth is hard to hear sometimes," I replied.

Clint jumped to his feet. His fists were clenched as he walked toward me, but Gage stopped him.

"No," he said sternly. "He'll get what's coming to him."

Clint didn't like it, but he reluctantly stopped.

"Tie him to that tree," Gage said. "Then we'd best turn in."

"With pleasure," Clint snarled.

He tied my hands behind my back again, and the knots were even tighter this time. Then he tied my legs together, and next he tied my torso to the tree. By the time he was finished, I could hardly move.

"Sleep well," he said sarcastically.

I decided it best not to answer.

Chapter forty

Lee and Brian arrived at Tomlin's headquarters just in time for supper. They tended to their horses, washed up, hurried to the main house, sat around the dinner table, and ate a hearty meal.

"How'd things go in town?" Mr. Tomlin asked.

"They went," Lee replied, his face dark.

Mr. Tomlin looked thoughtful, but he said no more about it.

April kept glancing at Lee, but he purposely avoided her gaze. That is, until after supper.

"Let's go outside," she said.

From her tone, Lee knew it wasn't a suggestion.

"Sure," he said.

They stepped out on the porch and sat. It was dark, and the cool breeze was pleasant.

They didn't talk for a while. They just sat beside each other, enjoying the moment.

"You don't hide your feelings so well," April finally said.

"How's that?" Lee looked at her.

"During supper, you looked like you had found half a worm in your apple."

"Sorry," Lee smiled faintly. "We had a rough day."

"June's been worried about you. She was sure relieved when you and Brian rode back in."

"Worried about what?"

"Last time you left, you didn't come back for months," April reminded.

Lee frowned at that but didn't say anything.

"So, what happened in town?" April urged.

Lee cleared his throat and started talking. He told her everything, and afterwards April was quiet while she took it all in.

Then she said, "My, my."

"That pretty much describes it," Lee said.

"What will you do now?"

"Get our hotel back."

"How?"

"How do you think?" Lee snorted.

April frowned and bit her lower lip.

"Isn't there another way?" She asked.

"There doesn't appear to be," Lee replied. "Ross is about as helpful as a burr under your saddle."

"You said Ed has four gun hands?"

"That we know of."

"And they're good?"

"They're alive, so they've been good enough."

"What's the plan?" April asked.

"Don't have one yet," Lee admitted. "But, Brian will think of something. He always does."

"I don't like this," April objected.

"Can't say I do either," Lee agreed. "But, it is what it is."

April didn't reply, and it was silent for a bit. Then a thought occurred to her, and an anxious look crossed her face.

"You could walk away," she suggested.

Lee was startled.

"And just let Ed have the hotel?" He asked, disapproval in his voice.

"Yes. Is it worth dying over?"

"Don't plan on dying."

April frowned, and tried another angle.

"But is it worth *killing* over?"

Lee pinched his face in thought.

"I think it is," he finally said. "It's our hotel. *Our* future. And we're right, and he's wrong."

April looked disappointed as she studied Lee's determined face.

"You won't change your mind," she said.

"'Fraid not," he shook his head.

"What if I asked you not to do this?"

A strained look crossed Lee's face.

"Please don't."

"But if I did?" April pressed.

Lee hesitated.

Then he said softly, "I'm not sure."

April looked hurt. She glanced away, and it was silent.

"At least I'm honest," Lee said after a moment.

"And I appreciate that," April said, then asked, "When will this happen?"

"We're in no hurry," Lee replied. "The longer we wait, the more nervous Ed will get."

"What will you do in the meantime?"

"Probably stay around here," Lee replied, then smiled. "June and I can play some more marbles."

"She'd like that."

"I'm going to beat her one of these days," Lee declared.

They both chuckled, anxious for a light moment. But then April's face turned dark as her thoughts returned to the hotel.

"These hired gun hands," she said. "Could they–," her voice trailed off.

"Kill me?" Lee finished her sentence.

She bit her lower lip again and nodded.

Lee considered the question, and then decided.

"No, they can't," he declared.

"How can you be so sure?" She looked up at him, her eyes wide and big.

"I just know."

"You're not just saying this to make me feel better?"

Lee was startled by the question. He frowned and squirmed in his chair.

"You ask difficult questions," he complained.

Part Four
"The Palace Hotel Robbery"

Chapter forty-one

It was a miserable night.

I didn't sleep much. By morning I was extremely stiff, and my fingers throbbed. My back was also out of sorts as a result of the odd position I was in.

It was still dark when I heard Gage and Clint stir. While Clint rekindled the fire and cooked breakfast, Gage saddled the horses.

From the corner of my eye, I also noticed that he saddled Little Man.

Breakfast smelled mighty good, but I wasn't offered any. In fact, they completely ignored me.

They talked in hushed voices while they ate. Then, I heard them moving about as they packed up camp.

Clint finally came over to me. He pulled out his knife, and he cut me loose from the tree and freed my legs. However, he left my hands tied.

"Get on your horse," he said.

"Are we going somewhere?" I asked.

"You'll find out soon enough," he growled. "Now move."

My legs were asleep, and it took me a moment to struggle to my feet. I swayed a bit, and then Clint shoved me in the direction of the horses.

I stumbled over to Little Man. I talked softly to him, and he backed his ears.

"Just like yesterday," I said softly.

"Quit stalling," Clint thumped me on the shoulder.

I ignored Clint and looked at Gage.

"I figured out your plan," I said, stalling for time.

Gage was rummaging through his saddlebags. He turned around, and he held a short quirt made from rawhide.

"That so?" He asked.

"You're going to make my horse buck through town, with me on him," I declared.

Gage looked pleased.

"You figured right," he said.

"It won't work," I declared.

"And why's that?" An amused look crossed Gage's face.

"It pains me to say this, but I can't ride him," I said truthfully.

"You'll stay on. Long enough anyway."

"How can you be so sure?" I asked, fearful of the answer.

"Clint's going to tie you to the saddle," Gage informed with pride.

"Feller could get killed that way," I objected.

"I know," Gage grinned wolfishly.

"He won't buck," I tried another angle. "You saw it. I rode it out of him."

"He will after a little encouragement."

Gage lifted the quirt, and Clint snickered.

There was no way out of it. So, I decided to change tactics and embrace the challenge.

"So, what's the plan?" I asked.

"You and Clint will circle town and come in from the other direction," Gage explained. "Meanwhile, I'll ride up the alley to the backside of the hotel. As soon as it gets daylight, Clint will turn you loose, encourage your horse a bit, fire a few shots in the air, and then git. I'll join him later."

I frowned in thought.

It wasn't all that bad a plan; I just wasn't too keen on being the bait.

"Kinrich would be proud," I admitted, and Gage grinned his pleasure.

"And that ain't all," he added.

"I think that's enough," I said, worried.

"You'll also have a noose around your neck," Gage informed. "When you finally fall off, you'll either be dragged to death or you'll break your neck."

"This day just keeps getting better," I said sarcastically.

"It's better than the bullet my son got," Gage said, anger in his voice.

"He earned that bullet," I said.

My comment angered them. Gage glared at me, and Clint clinched his fists.

I had nothing to lose, so I decided to add another log on the fire.

"You might as well know; I'll be coming for you," I said matter-of-factly.

Gage just stood there, thinking on that, and he chuckled gruffly.

"Mighty sure of yourself."

"That is correct," I said.

"I'll make it easy for you," Gage replied. "If you live through this, we'll be at Bigsley."

I nodded curtly.

Bigsley was a small mining town about a half-day's ride from Empty-lake. There was no law there yet, and it was a rough, booming place.

"I'll be there," I declared.

"We'll see," Gage grunted, and he turned toward his horse.

The conversation was over. Clint shoved me in the back, and with great difficulty I managed to get into the saddle.

I didn't say a word while Clint tied my feet to the stirrups. And, by the time he finished, there was no way I could get my feet out of the stirrups.

That was a bad feeling, and I felt a slight panic. But, I breathed deeply and managed to control my emotions.

Next, Clint pulled my rope off my saddle. He built a small loop and placed it around my neck, and then he tied the other end of my rope to my saddle horn. He coiled the slack and re-lashed my rope to my saddle.

"That should do it," he said.

Gage walked over, studied my predicament, and gave a satisfied grunt. He also gave the quirt to Clint, and then they mounted their horses.

"You watch him," Gage warned his son.

"I will."

"Be daylight soon. You'd best be on your way," Gage said, and he looked at me. "Enjoy your ride."

I didn't dare reply.

Clint snickered, grabbed my reins, and kicked up his horse.

Chapter forty-two

Clint didn't talk as we circled town.

I tried desperately to think my way out of this mess. However, being tied to the stirrups and having my hands bound severely limited my options.

There was a small cluster of trees next to the main road a short distance from town. Clint rode up amongst them and stopped. The sky in the east was just beginning to lighten, and we could make out the shapes of the buildings in town.

"We'll wait a few minutes," Clint said.

All I could do was nod.

Clint turned in the saddle and studied me, and there was no kindness in his face.

I'm going to enjoy this," he said.

I'm sure you will, I thought.

To my relief, Clint didn't say anything else. We just sat there, and time passed slowly as daylight arrived.

"It's time," Clint finally announced. He glanced at me and asked, "Any last words?"

I was silent.

"Nothing at all?"

I shook my head, and Clint narrowed his eyes.

"All right then," he snarled.

He dismounted, and I spotted the quirt in his hands. He walked over, and he looped my split reins around Little Man's neck and tied them together so they wouldn't drop.

"This is for Ryan," he said.

He raised the quirt, came down hard, and whipped Little Man viciously in the flank.

Little Man was taken by surprise. He leaped forward, let out a big windy, and took off in a dead run.

My body was snapped backwards, but I managed to recover. I leaned forward and squeezed the saddle with my legs as Little Man raced for town.

Three pistol shots sounded out behind me. That made Little Man run even harder, and already I could see town folks running out into the street to see what all the commotion was about.

As for me, I just held on as best as I could.

Chapter forty-three

Ed Hazel sat at his usual table in the corner of the hotel, eating breakfast.

Quirley and Chewy sat at a nearby table, looking bored. Quirley was rolling a smoke, and Chewy had a mouthful of tobacco.

They were men who craved action. But so far, all they'd done was sit around the hotel, keeping an eye on peaceful customers. They were ready for some excitement, and they were growing restless.

Ed was worried. He sensed that trouble was coming, and he wasn't quite sure what to do about it.

He had already sent Curt and Rod out to keep an eye on Lee and Brian, and they had ridden out over an hour ago.

Ed was sure that they would try something. Problem was, he had no idea what.

"Stay watchful today," Ed told his two gun hands. "Anything could happen."

"Sure," Quirley said.

Before Ed could reply, pistol shots sounded in the distance. Seconds later there were shouts from outside, followed by all sorts of commotion.

Ed jumped in his chair.

"What's going on?" He demanded.

Chewy and Quirley stood.

"Not sure, but *something's* happening," Quirley said.

"You two take a look," Ed said.

They were excited to be doing something, and they hurried toward the door before Ed could change his mind.

Ed watched them go. Then he stood and went to his office.

His mind was on other things, and he had already entered and shut the door before he noticed the broken glass in the window.

The back door was wide open. And there, standing beside his desk, was the older man that had shot Ross.

He held a pair of saddlebags. In the other hand was a Colt, and it was pointed at Ed.

"Don't make a sound," he said, his voice gentle.

"Who are you?" Ed's voice squeaked.

"We never introduced ourselves," the older man said. "I'm Gage Palmer. You remember me?"

"Yes."

"I said I'd be back."

"What do you want?" Ed managed to say.

"Open the safe. Now."

Ed was terrified, but he managed to control his emotions. He shook his head, and Gage frowned his displeasure.

"I won't ask again," he warned.

"I'm the only one who knows the combination," Ed lied. "You kill me, and you'll never open it."

"Maybe not, but I'll feel better."

Ed swallowed hard and shook his head stubbornly.

Gage scowled. He crossed the room with surprising quickness, and he struck Ed in the head with his Colt.

It was a stunning blow, and blood squirted from Ed's scalp. He fell to the floor, and Gage hit him again for good measure.

"Change your mind yet?"

Blood oozed down Ed's face. He nodded slightly, and Gage grunted his approval.

"Get moving," he said.

Ed staggered to his feet, swayed a bit, and moved to the safe.

Chapter forty-four

Little Man never offered to buck. Instead, he just ran wildly, and we flew down the main street.

My biggest worry was the rope around my neck. Some slack was working out of the coils, and it made a big loop down Little Man's side.

It would be a violent jerk if that slack were to hang on something. And, my neck would take the brunt of the punishment.

I wanted to shout whoa, but I knew better. Instead, all I could do was steer Little Man with my legs as best as I could.

Folks were shouting and running towards us, and Morgan got close enough to make an attempt to grab my reins. But he missed, stumbled, and almost fell down.

It looked as if Little Man was going to race through town and keep going. But then, he stumped his toe and stumbled. He regained his balance and slid to an abrupt halt.

He just stood there, breathing heavily. As for me, I didn't say a word as folks approached us.

Several of the men surrounded Little Man, and some of them pulled out their knifes.

I felt Little Man flinch, and I swallowed hard and said a silent prayer.

"Easy boys," I heard Morgan say. "Somebody grab that horse."

A tall, skinny man grabbed the reins, and I heaved an inward sigh of relief.

The men with knives came up beside me and started cutting me loose. Meanwhile, everyone else started asking questions all at once.

"Rondo! What happened? Who did this to you? Where'd you get that horse? Why are you all tied up? Are you all right? Why aren't you talking?" They asked.

I didn't dare reply. I just stared at them, waiting.

"He must be in shock," Morgan suggested, and everybody nodded their agreement.

It seemed like it took them forever to cut me loose.

As soon as I could move, I reached up and pulled the rope off my neck. Then I dismounted, and it took a moment for my legs to quit trembling.

By now the questions had stopped. Everybody just stared at me, waiting for me to say something.

I looked around, and I was surprised by the size of the crowd.

I grunted.

Gage's plan worked, I thought.

I took several deep breaths and gathered myself. Then, I turned and patted Little Man on the neck.

"Thanks, boy," I whispered in his ear.

He backed his ears in response while I turned to the crowd.

All three city council members were close by, and I looked at them and cleared my throat.

"I'll take that job now," I said.

"Sure," Morgan agreed, then asked, "But what happened?"

I ignored his question.

"I need a gun," I said. Nobody replied, so I added, "Now."

"Take mine," Morgan offered, and he unbuckled his gun belt and handed it over.

I strapped it on, palmed the Colt, and made sure it was loaded. Then I walked toward the hotel, and everybody followed a short distance behind me.

There were two, rough looking, tobacco smelling men on the porch. They watched me silently as I walked up.

I studied them a moment, then asked, "Who are you?"

"We work for Ed," the one with a cigarette said.

"And where is Ed?"

"Probably in his office."

"I was afraid of that," I said, and I pushed through the batwing doors.

Chapter forty-five

We found Ed in his office.

He was sitting on the floor beside the safe, holding his head. Blood dribbled off his chin and splattered on the floor.

The safe was wide open; it was empty.

Folks poured into the office. Everyone started asking questions, and it got noisy.

The back door was wide open. I walked out and looked down the alley, but Gage was already long gone.

I sighed my displeasure, turned, and went back inside.

Everyone was still demanding answers, but Ed just sat there looking dazed.

Since I was the sheriff now, I decided to take charge.

"Quiet!" I raised my voice.

Everyone hushed down and gave me a hurt look.

"Everybody out," I ordered.

"Who made you boss?" An angry citizen said.

I looked at everyone a moment.

Then I said, "I'm the sheriff."

As soon as I said that, Ed glanced up sharply. But then he winced as his head hurt.

Nobody liked it, but everyone left the room. That is, all except the city council members and Ed's two gun hands.

I frowned at them, but they stared at me with blank faces.

"Who are you two again?" I asked.

"We work for Ed," the one with a cigarette repeated.

"So you said," I said. "You got a name?"

They were in no hurry to reply. The one with a cigarette took in a long drag and then exhaled.

"I'm Quirley," he finally said. "This is Chewy."

We stared at each other a moment. Then I turned and looked at Ed.

I already knew who I was after, but I figured I should ask a few questions anyhow.

"Did you get a look at the man who hit you?" I asked.

Ed shook his head.

"Not much I can recall," he said, his voice weak. "He forced me to open the safe."

"I sorta figured that."

"Once I opened it, he hit me again, and I passed out for a second. When I came to, he had already filled his saddlebags. Then he went out the back door."

"Shocking," I said.

It was silent a moment. I watched Ed, and he seemed to be thinking hard. Then his face lit up, as if something suddenly occurred to him.

"Actually, I *did* get a good look at him," he announced.

I frowned at that.

"You just said you didn't," I reminded.

"I misunderstood your question."

I doubted that, but I decided to let it go.

"All right," I said. "What'd he look like?"

"It was Lee Mattingly," he declared.

To say I was shocked was an understatement. My mouth fell open, and I stared at Ed with a dumbfounded look.

"What?"

"It was Lee," Ed repeated.

The three city council members murmured amongst themselves. Meanwhile, I just stood there in confusion.

"You're mistaken," I said.

"I know what I saw," Ed glared at me.

I was at a loss for words. I just stared at Ed, and he stared back.

My mind raced, but I couldn't think of anything to say.

"Thanks for the information," I finally said, and I started to walk out.

"Rondo," Fred Stilwell called out.

"Yes?" I stopped and looked back.

"I hate to mention it, but it's your duty to find and arrest Lee and Brian."

"I know my job," I said bluntly.

"The last time they were in trouble with the law, you allowed them to escape," Fred reminded.

I studied everyone for a moment.

Then I said, "I'll get the men who robbed the hotel."

I turned and walked out before anyone could reply.

Chapter forty-six

I went down the street to the sheriff's office. I walked in abruptly, and I was surprised to see Ross sitting behind the desk.

He was just as surprised to see me.

"What are you doing here?" He demanded.

"Long story," I replied. I studied him a moment, and added, "You look better than yesterday."

"That's 'cause I *feel* better."

"Glad to hear that."

"What's all the commotion outside?" Ross changed the subject. "I heard shots."

"The Palace Hotel was robbed, among other things," I announced.

To my surprise, Ross didn't seem all that excited. He nodded and chuckled gruffly.

"Lee and Brian work fast," he said.

I was startled.

"Lee and Brian?" I narrowed my eyes.

"Sure," Ross nodded. "They all but told me they were planning on robbing the hotel. Something to do with a contract."

I was so confused, I didn't know where to start. I decided not to even try.

"I don't know about that," I responded. "But Lee and Brian didn't rob the hotel. Gage Palmer did."

"Who's that?"

"The feller that shot you," I said, and then I asked, "Where's Lee and Brian? I need to find them."

"Probably at the Tomlin's ranch."

"Good," I said.

I unbuckled Morgan's gun belt and placed it on the desk. Then I walked over to the gun cabinet, pulled out an extra gun belt and revolver, strapped it on, and handled the Colt some.

"Did you lose your ivory handled Colt?" Ross asked as he watched me.

"Just for a little while," I replied, and then I nodded at Morgan's Colt. "Will you see that Morgan gets this back?"

"I can do that."

"'Preciate it."

Ross nodded, and I headed for the door. I started to walk out, but I stopped when a thought occurred to me.

"I took the sheriff's job," I announced.

"I sorta figured that," Ross smiled weakly.

"No hard feelings?"

"Nope."

"Thanks, Ross."

"Are you still heading to Midway?" Ross wanted to know.

"Sooner or later," I replied. "I've got some things to take care of first."

"When you do head out, mind if I ride along?"

My face filled with concern.

"Sure you're up to it?"

"I'm ready to leave now," Ross replied.

I studied his determined look and nodded.

"All right then," I said.

Ross grinned, and I was glad to see it. I smiled back and walked out.

Part Five
"Bigsley and Conclusion"

Chapter forty-seven

I walked down the street toward Little Man.

Now that the excitement had faded, things in town were returning to their normal routine.

There were two youngsters painting our house, and they didn't look very enthused about it. I stopped and watched them, and they spotted me after a moment.

"Help you, Sheriff?" One of them asked sarcastically, and I suddenly realized that the youth was Fred Stilwell's son.

I ignored the question.

"Missed a spot," I pointed.

He looked to where I was pointing and scowled.

"And quit dripping paint on the porch," I added.

I walked on before he could reply. I reached Little Man, untied him from the hitching post, and stepped into the saddle.

Fred's son was still standing there, looking scornfully at me. I motioned for him to get back to work, and his scowl deepened as he turned and grabbed his paintbrush.

I smiled and kicked Little Man up to a trot.

***

About a mile out, I spotted two riders riding toward town.

They rode with ease and purpose, and my curiosity was kindled. But, I had other things to worry about, so I didn't think on them long.

Things looked peaceful at the ranch, and as I rode up I spotted Rachel sitting out on the porch. Lee, Brian, April, and June were also on the porch, and they all looked surprised to see me.

The sight of my wife made my heart leap with joy, especially when Rachel uttered a gasp of surprise.

"Rondo!" She called out. "What are you doing here?"

I almost replied, but I stopped myself just in time. I dismounted, and Rachel rushed into my arms before I could tie Little Man to the hitching rail. It didn't matter, because Little Man just stood there, his head down, lazily twitching his tail.

We embraced and kissed. Then I reluctantly let her go, and we walked hand in hand to the porch.

As usual, Lee was studying the situation with keen eyes. First, he noticed my Colt, and then he studied Little Man.

"Make a horse trade?" He asked, and his eyes twinkled.

"More or less," I said.

There was a pot of coffee on the porch, and my mouth salivated when I caught a whiff of it. I suddenly realized just how hungry I was.

"Coffee smells good," I hinted.

Rachel poured me a cup. I sat in a chair, took a swig, and sighed in contentment.

"Ma is cooking lunch," Rachel said, reading my thoughts.

"I could eat," I smiled at her.

"While we're waiting, why don't you tell us what happened to you?" Lee suggested.

I nodded. I took another swig of coffee, collected my thoughts, and started talking.

Chapter forty-eight

I took my time and told them everything. That is, everything except Little Man bucking me off. I figured that could stay between Little Man and me.

Lee and Brian looked startled when I told them about the hotel being robbed, and afterwards everybody was quiet while they took in everything.

"Let me get this straight," Lee finally said. "Everybody thinks Brian and I robbed the hotel."

"Yep, even Ross thinks so."

Lee chuckled and shook his head.

"How 'bout that," he said softly.

"And, everyone expects me to arrest you two and bring you in," I announced.

"Think you could do it?" Lee looked amused.

"I've got better things to do," I declared.

"Like what?" Lee looked curious.

"I'm going after Gage and Clint Palmer," I informed, and there was anger in my voice.

"Sounds personal," Lee observed.

"I'm the sheriff now. It's my job," I reminded.

"That's it?" Lee watched me closely.

"What else is there?" I asked sharply.

Lee smiled knowingly and let it go. I scowled at him, and decided to change the subject.

"I've got a question," I said. "Several, in fact."

"You usually do," Lee's smile lingered.

"Why does everyone think you and Brian robbed the hotel?"

"You know how it is," Lee shrugged.

"How *what* is?"

"We always get blamed for *everything*."

"Sure you do," I said.

Lee didn't reply, and I waited.

April sighed and scowled at Lee.

"You might as well tell him," she scolded.

Lee grinned. He cleared his throat, and then he told me everything that had happened while I was gone. And, by the time he finished, everything made sense.

"I leave for *one* day," I said, shaking my head, "and everything falls apart."

"What would we do without you?" Lee jested.

"Were you *really* going to rob the hotel?" I asked disapprovingly.

"We'll never know," Lee grinned.

I grunted in response, and then I frowned as my thoughts returned to Ed.

"He might not look like much, but Ed is smart," I said. "He's handling this like a game of chess, more or less."

"And, he has more pieces to move around the board than we do," Lee added. "He's got four experienced gun hands working for him."

"I met two of them, and I think I saw the other two riding in," I recalled.

"I don't understand why Ed's putting the blame on us," Brian spoke up.

"He wants you and Lee out of the way," I explained. "It'd be his word against yours at the trial, and you two are ex-outlaws."

"So, in order to get us out of the way, Ed would allow Gage and Clint to escape?" Brian asked, confused.

"Not hardly," I replied. "I'm sure he's already sent a couple of his gun hands out to find their tracks."

Lee and Brian didn't like that. They glanced at each other, and then Brian looked at me.

"You're sure there weren't any files in the safe?" He asked.

"It was empty," I confirmed.

"So, Gage and Clint have the contract," Brian surmised.

"It would appear so," I agreed.

130

"Well then," Lee spoke up. "We need to find Gage and Clint *before* Ed does."

"We will," I said.

"You seem confident," Lee studied me.

"That's 'cause I am," I said, and explained. "I know where they're headed."

Lee and Brian jumped in surprise, and then Lee scowled at me.

"You didn't mention that," he muttered.

"I reckon you'd like to come along?" I asked innocently.

"We would."

"That's fine," I said, then added, "It'll have to be legal, though."

"What will?" Lee and Brian looked confused.

"I'm not sure of the words, but you two had better raise your hands and say 'I do,'" I said.

"'I do' to what?" Lee demanded.

"To be my special deputies," I announced.

"Not again," Lee objected. "You'll ruin our reputations for sure."

"One can only hope."

Lee and Brian glanced at each other; then looked back at me.

"Fine," Lee grumbled.

They raised their hands and solemnly said, "I do."

"Consider yourselves deputies," I grinned.

They didn't share my enthusiasm.

"Whoop-de-do," Lee replied sourly.

Chapter forty-nine

Supper was ready, so we stood and started to go inside.

I glanced at Rachel. To my surprise, she had her arms crossed and looked unhappy.

"Go ahead," I told everyone else. "We'll be there in a minute."

Lee glanced at Rachel, smiled knowingly, and led everyone in.

"What's the matter?" I asked Rachel as soon as we were alone.

"You took the sheriff's job without even talking to me," she pouted.

That thought hadn't occurred to me, and I frowned thoughtfully.

"I reckon I did," I admitted. "Things just happened so fast."

"And now you're the sheriff again."

"I am," I admitted.

Rachel studied my face.

"Is this what you want?" She asked.

It was silent as I considered that, and then I nodded.

"Yes, I think it is."

"But it's dangerous work," she objected.

"I'm good at dangerous."

"All it takes is once," Rachel warned.

"I know that," I said.

"And, you're about to be a father," she continued.

"I know that too."

"Did you think about that while you were gone?" Rachel wanted to know.

"I sure did," I declared.

"And?" She urged.

"Let's have another one as soon as possible," I said, excitement in my voice.

"What?" Her mouth fell open.

"A little boy needs a brother," I explained. "Or a sister."

Rachel was surprised. She almost smiled, but she caught herself just in time.

"He'll need a father too," she tried to be stern.

"He has one," I declared.

Rachel studied me a moment.

Then she said, "All right then."

We kissed and went inside for supper.

Chapter fifty

We turned in early.

I was still sore after all I'd gone through, and it felt good to sleep on a bed.

We were up early, ate breakfast, and had our horses saddled before sunrise. Mr. Tomlin offered me a fresh mount, but I decided to ride Little Man.

"That is the ugliest horse I ever saw," Lee commented.

"Is," I agreed. "But, he's got heart."

Lee grunted, but I ignored him as I went to tell Rachel goodbye.

Lee wasn't far behind me. While I talked to Rachel, he said goodbye to April and June.

"Please be careful," Rachel said wistfully.

"Always," I replied.

"We'll be here, waiting for you."

"I'll be back as soon as I can," I promised.

We embraced and kissed. Then I let her go and walked toward Little Man.

"Rondo," Rachel stopped me.

"Yes?" I looked back.

"Go get 'em."

"I will," I said.

***

We climbed on our horses and took out in a brisk trot.

Bigsley was to the southwest, and I figured we would arrive late afternoon.

We traveled in silence, and by midmorning we had traveled several miles. I led the way, and Little Man traveled in an easy trot.

"How much further is it?" Lee broke the silence.

I started to reply, but I caught myself just in time. I looked back at Lee and shrugged.

"You don't know?" Lee shot me an odd look.

I sighed, pulled up, and dismounted.

"We should be there this evening," I said.

"Why didn't you say so?" Lee grumbled.

I didn't reply as Lee and Brian dismounted. We sat under the shade of a nearby tree, uncapped our canteens, and took several swigs.

I thought the situation over, and I sighed irritably.

So far, I had avoided mentioning how I couldn't talk on Little Man. But, it was obvious they had to know.

"It's a hard thing to admit," I broke the silence.

"What is?" Lee looked at me.

"I've been busting broncs all my life," I declared.

"I know that," Lee said.

"I've never come across one I couldn't ride, until now."

"Oh?" Lee raised an eyebrow.

I nodded and gestured at Little Man, who was just standing there ground reined, half asleep.

"*Him*?" Lee made a face.

"Yep."

"Surely not," Lee tried not to laugh.

"Can't ride him," I admitted softly.

"But you've been on him all day," Lee objected.

"Sure," I said. "As long as I don't talk, he won't do anything."

Lee stared at me as if I were crazy.

"Watch this," I said, and I stood and walked over to Little Man.

I talked to him, and he backed his ears as usual.

"See?" I said. "And when I'm on him, he explodes."

Lee frowned and scratched his jaw.

"Never heard of such a thing," he said.

"You're welcome to climb on and see for yourself," I offered.

"I'll take your word on it," Lee flashed me a smile.

Brian cleared his throat. We glanced at him, and he had his brow wrinkled in thought.

"There was this old-timer once-," Brian started to say.

"Older than you?" Lee cut in.

"Yes, much older."

"He really *was* an old-timer," Lee jested.

Brian frowned at him, and then continued.

"I recall him saying he had a similar experience," he said. "He had a horse, real gentle like, that all of a sudden started bucking. He'd rub and paw at his ears, and act real peculiar when folks talked around him."

"What was wrong with him?" I asked.

"The old-timer figured he had an ear infection of some sort," Brian replied. "He poured some whiskey in his ears, and he got better after a dose or two."

I frowned thoughtfully.

"That's it?"

"Well, that's all I can remember."

"I'll have to try that."

"At least you could talk," Lee pointed out.

"Be helpful," I replied.

We all took another swig of water, recapped our canteens, stepped into our saddles, and kicked up our horses.

Chapter fifty-one

Now that Lee knew about Little Man, he tried relentlessly to coax me to talk. He told jokes and asked question after question.

I never replied; I just smiled good-naturedly.

The day wore on.

So far, the country around us had been flat, with a few gentle rolling hills, some mesquite bushes, and a few trees scattered about.

By early afternoon, the terrain started getting rougher. There were more rocks, and a long, steep mesa spread out in front of us.

There was a worn trail that led to the top, and it weaved back and forth.

It took us an hour to reach the top, and from there we could see the country a long ways in all directions.

Our horses were breathing hard, so we dismounted and let them catch their wind. Lee looked around some, and I rummaged through my saddlebags, pulled out my spyglass, and squinted through it.

There, in the distance, was the small town of Bigsley.

"There it is," I announced.

I looked at Lee. He was a short distance away, studying the ground.

"Somebody camped up here last night," he announced.

He squatted on his heels beside an old campfire. He felt the coals and grunted in satisfaction.

"Still a mite warm," he said.

"Reckon it was Gage and Clint?" Brian asked.

"Sure possible," I said.

"As long as they're in Bigsley, I don't reckon it matters," Lee replied.

"Reckon so," I agreed.

Lee walked back over to us, and we stood there a moment and took in the view.

I don't know why, but I turned, brought up the spyglass, and studied our back trail.

I swept the countryside, and I suddenly grunted in surprise.

"What is it?" Brian asked.

"Two riders," I announced. "Riding this way, real slow like, as if they're following tracks."

"Recognize them?" Lee asked.

"Nope."

"Let me see," Lee said.

I handed him the spyglass, and Lee squinted through it.

Several seconds passed. Then Lee breathed deeply and heaved a sigh.

"I was afraid of that," he said, his voice flat.

"You know 'em?"

"Sure do."

"Who is it?" I urged.

He lowered the eyeglass, glanced at Brian, and then looked at me.

"The Window Brothers," he said softly.

Chapter fifty-two

I was confused.

"Window Brothers?" I repeated.

"Curt 'n Rod Tisdale," Lee explained. "They work for Ed."

"Clever," I smiled.

"We liked it."

"I've heard of them," I said thoughtfully. "They ain't amateurs."

"Nope, they're not," Lee confirmed.

"What are we going to do?" Brian spoke up.

I thought on that, then said, "Only one thing *to* do."

"And what's that?" Brian looked at me.

"Get there first."

"Then what?"

"We'll apprehend Gage and Clint," I declared.

"What about the money from the hotel?" Brian wanted to know.

"We'll apprehend that too," I said.

"The Window Brothers will be after it," Lee warned.

"Well, they can't have it."

"They won't like that," Lee said.

"Don't imagine they will," I agreed.

"Could be a problem," Lee surmised, and he suddenly looked wistful.

"Could be," I nodded.

Lee took in a deep breath and exhaled slowly.

"They ain't bad fellows," he said.

"Who? The Window Brothers?" I asked.

Lee nodded and said, "Can't explain it really. They're just likeable."

"Well, likeable or not, we'll have to deal with them," I said.

"Yes," Lee said slowly. "We will."

"Well then," I suggested. "We'd best git before they catch up."

Lee nodded, and we walked toward our horses.

Chapter fifty-three

We made our way down the mesa and trotted towards Bigsley. We arrived about a half hour before dark.

Bigsley wasn't very impressive. However, most boomtowns never are.

There were only a dozen or so buildings.

They weren't very well built, but that didn't seem to matter to anybody. There was a boarding house, a few eating establishments, a livery stable, and of course, a saloon.

There were more buildings being built further down the street, and folks hustled all about.

The feeling grabbed ahold of me as we walked our horses down the main street. Just like that I felt calm, steady, and ready.

I also felt a deep, burning rage.

Gage and Clint's main purpose in life was to kill me. I suddenly realized when they learned I was alive they would no doubt try again. If I didn't end it here, it could put my family at risk, and I couldn't allow that to happen.

"Busy place," Lee interrupted my thoughts.

I was on Little Man, so I just nodded.

We pulled up and dismounted beside the livery stable. There was a tall, thin man hurrying by, and I called out to him.

He stopped and scowled at us.

"What do you want?" He demanded roughly.

I ignored his sarcasm and smiled pleasantly.

"You got a name?" I asked.

"Who wants to know?" He snorted.

"Rondo Landon," I announced in a soft voice.

His eyes grew wide, and his mood changed instantly.

"Rondo Landon!" He exclaimed. "I've heard of you!"

"Most have."

A few seconds passed. I just stood there, looking at him, and waited.

He swallowed and said, "I'm Willis. I don't want any trouble."

I nodded curtly.

"Willis, we're looking for two fellers that rode in earlier," I said. "One is older than the other."

He suddenly seemed eager to help.

"Sure, I saw them," he said. "They got a room at the boarding house."

"Where are they now?"

"In the saloon."

"Care to do me a favor?" I asked, and I reached into my pocket, pulled out a dollar coin, and tossed it him.

"Sure," he replied.

"Go to the saloon and tell them I'd like to see them," I said. "I'll be in the street."

His eyes widened some more.

"Is there going to be trouble?"

"Sure possible," I said, then urged, "Go on now."

"Yes, sir," he said.

Willis hurried down the street and disappeared inside the saloon. Meanwhile, we tied our horses to a nearby hitching post and checked our weapons.

"How you want to handle this," Lee said as we holstered our Colts.

"You two stay here," I replied.

"There's two of them," Lee objected.

"I know."

Lee studied my face and frowned.

"I thought you said this wasn't personal," he reminded.

"I changed my mind," I said.

Chapter fifty-four

Lee scowled, but I ignored him as I walked down the street.

I stopped about thirty feet from the saloon. Then I just stood there and waited.

A long minute passed, and Gage and Clint stepped out. They walked out into the street and stopped in front of me.

Gage stared at me with stern, thoughtful eyes. Clint meanwhile, displayed an arrogant smirk on his face. His hand hovered over his Colt's handle, and his fingers twitched in anticipation.

"You're still alive," Gage spoke, his voice gentle.

"Sorry to disappoint you," I said.

"How'd you get out of it?"

"I kept my mouth shut."

Gage didn't understand that, and he frowned thoughtfully.

"Ryan always said you were lucky," he scoffed.

"Not so much," I corrected. "Ryan was the lucky one."

"Until you killed him," Gage said.

I shrugged.

"His luck finally ran out."

Anger flashed in Gage's eyes. I thought he was about to draw, but instead he looked past me.

"You brought help."

"My deputies," I explained. "Lee Mattingly and Brian Clark."

Recognition flashed across his face.

"Heard of them," he said. "They rode with Kinrich."

"That's right," I said. "We're all that's left."

"They quit on Kinrich too," Gage said, anger in his voice.

"Well, some of us were smarter than others."

Gage narrowed his eyes at that, but didn't reply.

I took advantage of the silence and changed the subject.

"You robbed the hotel," I accused.

"We did," he admitted.

"I'm here to take you back," I announced.

"What for?"

"Because I'm the sheriff."

Gage was surprised.

"That happened fast," he said.

"Job was available. I took it," I explained.

"I see."

"Unbuckle your gun belts and then raise your hands," I said. "Nobody has to die."

Gage smiled at that, and he shook his head slightly.

"Can't do that," he said gently.

"I know, but I still had to say it," I said.

He didn't reply, and a heavy silence filled the street.

There was no need to say more. We just stood there, looking at each other, and my hand hovered patiently over my Colt's handle.

I watched Gage's eyes. They blinked suddenly, and he made a grab for his Colt.

I palmed my Colt and fired before he even touched his handle. My aim was true, and my bullet struck him in his torso and flipped him over backwards.

I turned to Clint.

He was just bringing his Colt up. He fired too soon, and his bullet hit the ground and whined as it ricocheted.

I fired twice before he could recover.

My first bullet struck him in his midsection; my second took him in his chest.

Clint dropped his Colt, staggered backwards, clutched at his chest, and fell over. He kicked out a few times, and then was still.

After that I just stood there, looking at them. Neither one moved, so I reloaded my Colt and holstered it.

Chapter fifty-five

I heard footsteps behind me. Lee and Brian walked up, and their faces were grim.

"You all right?" Lee asked.

"I reckon," I said, my voice flat.

Lee studied me a moment. Then he walked over and looked down at Clint.

"Looks just like his brother," he commented.

"Shoots like him too," Brian added.

Lee smiled at that and looked at me.

"You're faster now than you ever was," he declared.

I didn't feel like discussing it, so I just shrugged.

"You need us for anything?" Lee asked.

"Not particularly," I replied.

Lee nodded, and he and Brian hurried toward the boarding house. Meanwhile, I looked down at the bodies and frowned in thought.

I looked up and spotted Willis watching me from the shadows of the saloon.

"Willis," I waved him over.

"Yes?"

I dug in my pocket, pulled out several dollar coins, and gave them to him.

"Go saddle their horses," I said. "And, find some tarps we can wrap them up in."

He stuffed the money in his pocket, nodded, and scampered away.

A few minutes passed, and I spotted Lee and Brian walking towards me. Lee carried a pair of saddlebags, and they looked pleased.

"Find the money?" I asked.

"Sure did," Brian said, and he waved a piece of paper at me. "And here's the contract. Signed and everything."

"Ed's name ain't on it," Lee added.

"Congratulations," I said.

"I figured you might want this back," Lee held up my gun belt.

"You figured right," I said.

He handed it over, and I pulled out my ivory handled Colt and looked it over. There wasn't a scratch on it, and I smiled.

"What happens to the money?" Brian asked me.

I shrugged.

"It belongs to the hotel," I said.

Lee and Brian were silent as they thought on that.

"But the hotel belongs to us," Lee finally said.

"Reckon it does," I agreed.

Lee and Brian glanced at each other and grinned. Meanwhile, I unbuckled the gun belt I had on and strapped mine on. I made sure my Colt was loaded, and then I holstered it.

Lee was watching me.

"Feel better?" He asked.

"Does," I replied with a smile.

Chapter fifty-six

Willis came down the street, leading two saddled horses behind him.

He also had some tarps, and we rolled Gage and Clint up into them.

After that, we turned our attention to the horses. It took a bit, but we managed to get Gage and Clint laid across the saddles and tied down.

"Horses are a bit skittish," Lee commented.

"I reckon they're used to folks riding them head up instead of head down," I replied.

Lee nodded and asked, "We riding out tonight?"

"Be safer than staying in town," I reasoned. "Especially with all that money."

"Don't forget about the Window Brothers," Lee warned. "They'll be showing up soon."

"Yes, we can't forget about them," I agreed.

"Might be best if we dealt with them here, instead of out there," Lee suggested.

"What do you have in mind?" I asked.

A wistful look crossed Lee's face.

"Might not make any difference," he said. "But, I'd like to talk to them."

"About what?"

"See if they'll listen to reason."

"If they don't?" I asked.

"Then they don't."

I nodded thoughtfully.

"All right then," I said.

***

I told Willis to stash Gage and Clint at the livery stable. He wasn't too keen on the idea, but he changed his mind when I paid him a few more dollars.

"Keep an eye out," I told him. "When you see two riders coming in, tell them we're waiting at the saloon."

"More trouble?" Willis asked, excited.

"Perhaps," I said, then added, "Go on now."

Willis nodded and led the horses down the street.

We watched him leave, and then we went to the saloon. We walked in, allowed our eyes to adjust, and took a slow look around.

It was a dark, smoke filled, musky room. All talking stopped when we were spotted, and everybody stared curiously at us.

I cleared my throat.

"I'm Rondo Landon," I announced. Nobody replied, so I added, "There's a good possibility trouble's coming."

"Coming where?" A man at the bar asked.

"Right here," I pointed at the floor of the saloon.

No one needed any more encouragement. Everybody finished their drinks with haste and headed for the door.

"That didn't take long," Lee said once we were alone.

"Didn't," I agreed.

We familiarized ourselves with the room. A few minutes passed, and we heard running footsteps from outside. The batwing doors burst open, and Willis appeared.

"Don't shoot!" He said, then added, "They just rode in."

"You tell them?" I asked.

Willis nodded.

"They said they'd be along."

I glanced at Lee and Brian, and then looked back at Willis.

"Then you'd best git," I suggested.

Chapter fifty-seven

I walked over and stood in the corner, and I was partly hidden by dark shadows. Brian stayed across the room, and he leaned against the bar. He held his shotgun, and he pulled both triggers back.

Lee sat at a table in the middle of the room, facing the doors.

He rummaged through the saddlebags. He carefully stacked a pile of cash on the table, and he placed the contract beside the pile. Then, he stashed the saddlebags underneath the table.

After that, we just waited.

Time passed slowly, and tension built. Then there was movement at the door, and in stepped two men.

They were just as Lee had described. They were watchful, and they studied the room with care.

The shortest one, which I figured was Rod, gazed at Brian, then at Lee. He looked at me last, and he studied me with a professional carefulness.

"You with them?" He asked.

"I am," I replied.

"You must be Rondo," he figured.

"That's right."

He seemed pleased.

"Heard of you."

"Lot of folks have," I said.

"You heard of us?"

"Yes."

"They say you're the fastest gun around."

"Depends on who's around," I shrugged.

Rod liked that.

He smiled and said, "Perhaps we'll see."

"Perhaps," I agreed.

His eyes twinkled as he glanced at Lee.

"Lee," he said.

"Rod," Lee replied.

"I reckon you know why we're here."

"Reckon I do," Lee said.

"Smart, spreading out like that," Rod commented.

"Is, ain't it."

"What's the money for?" Rod nodded at the table.

"It's for you," Lee announced.

Rod chuckled and shook his head.

"We already discussed this. We work for Ed."

"No, you work for the hotel," Lee corrected.

"Same thing."

"Not anymore."

"And how's that?" Rod looked amused.

Lee tapped the contract with his finger.

"Brian and I are the legal owners of the hotel," he said. "This signed contract proves it."

Rod frowned at that. He glanced at Curt, then at me.

Then he shrugged and said, "Doesn't matter who owns the hotel. We still work for Ed."

"Good luck getting paid," Lee said. "Ed's broke."

Rod considered that, then said, "He won't be when we get his money back."

"You figure on taking all three of us?" Lee objected.

Rod glanced around the room but didn't say anything.

"You can die here," Lee continued. "Or, you can take this cash as payment for your services and ride out."

"You have this all figured out," Rod said.

"I try."

"And if we refuse?"

"We'll arrest you," I spoke up.

"On what charge?" Rod challenged.

"I'll think of something," I said.

Rod chuckled, but not humorously. It was silent, and I could tell they were thinking it over.

"Way I see it, is you were lied to," Lee said.

"How's that," Rod said.

"Ed never owned the hotel. He's been trying to steal it from us all along."

"One way to look at it," Rod said.

"Is," Lee agreed.

Rod took in a deep breath and heaved a sigh. He glanced at his brother, and I saw Curt give a slight nod.

They looked at each other a moment. Then Rod returned the nod and looked at Lee.

"We ain't afraid of you," he said.

"I know," Lee said.

"But, like you said, we work for the hotel."

"And Ed doesn't own the hotel," Lee reminded. "We do."

"So, we'll ride on," Rod announced.

A relieved look crossed Lee's face.

"Glad to hear that," he said.

"Worried?" Rod smiled.

"Just didn't want to kill you," Lee returned the smile.

"Sorta glad we don't have to kill you neither," Rod chuckled. Then his face turned serious, and he added, "Doesn't mean there won't be a time."

"I know," Lee said softly.

Rod nodded. Then, while Curt stayed by the door, Rod walked to the table and collected the cash.

"Well, I reckon this is goodbye," Rod said.

"I reckon it is," Lee agreed.

"We've enjoyed our, uh, *conversations*," Rod's eyes twinkled.

"So have I," Lee said.

"Maybe we'll come visit you at the hotel sometime," Rod suggested.

"Come by anytime," Lee offered.

Rod nodded, and then he glanced at me.

Several seconds passed while we looked at each other. Then he said, "Nice meeting you."

"You too," I said.

"Fastest gun around," he commented. He chuckled at that and joined his brother at the door.

"Rod," Lee said.

"Yes?" Rod looked back at him.

"I just have to ask," Lee said. "Anybody ever call you the Window Brothers?"

Rod looked puzzled.

"No. Why?"

"Curt 'n Rod," Lee explained.

It was silent, and then Rod laughed. They obviously thought it was funny, because even Curt chuckled.

"We might have to use that," Rod mused.

"Be my guest," Lee offered.

Rod was still chuckling as they turned toward the door.

"Take care," he said.

"We will," Lee said.

Then they pushed through the batwing doors and were gone.

Chapter fifty-eight

Our business in Bigsley was complete, so we prepared to leave.

While Lee tied the saddlebags on behind his saddle, I went to the livery stable and collected Gage and Clint. Then we stepped into our saddles and rode out. I led Gage's horse, and Brian led Clint's.

I could tell Lee was pleased. I understood why he liked the Window Brothers, and I was glad we avoided bloodshed.

It was a good feeling. However, Gage and Clint ruined any triumph I felt.

I always felt a little nauseous and depressed after a gunfight. It wasn't that I felt guilty. I just disliked killing, even if they deserved it.

Lee and Brian must have known how I felt, because they left me alone.

By now it was dark. But the moon was full, and we could see the ground good enough.

We traveled in an easy trot, and it didn't take us long to reach the mesa. We nudged our horses forward and started climbing. It was steep going, and Gage was about to slide off his horse by the time we reached the top.

I dismounted and tied Gage back in place. Then I looked at Lee and Brian.

"Be a good place to stop," I suggested.

"I could drink some coffee," Lee replied.

I nodded my agreement, and they dismounted and gathered some loose mesquite wood while I tended to the horses.

I didn't take the time to unpack Gage and Clint. I just left them in their saddles, and I picketed their horses so they could graze.

I joined Lee and Brian, and we sat around the campfire and waited for the coffee to boil. As soon as it was ready, we filled our cups and leaned back.

We didn't talk much. Instead, we just sat there, taking occasional swigs and thinking our own thoughts.

After a while, Lee pulled out a cigar. He bit off the end, struck a match, and lit it. He took a deep puff, and then looked at me.

"Ed's going to be upset," he said.

"Just a little," I agreed.

"He'll probably have Quirley and Chewy try to kill us."

"We can handle them."

Lee's face turned wistful.

"I wish there was another way," he said softly.

"Like what?" I pressed.

"Not sure exactly," Lee admitted. "But just once, I'd like to solve things-," he paused while he searched for the right word, "-tactfully."

"No need to be tactful when we can outshoot them," Brian pointed out.

Lee frowned at that, and it was silent a moment. I studied Lee's face, and then I cleared my throat.

"What's this really about?" I asked.

Lee took another puff on his cigar and exhaled slowly.

"April," he admitted.

"What about her?" I asked.

"She doesn't want me killing anybody over the hotel. She says it isn't worth it."

I nodded my understanding and scratched my jaw in thought.

"But sometimes, folks *need* killing," I pointed out.

"I know that."

"However," I thought it over. "Ed hasn't exactly done anything wrong yet. But, he won't give up the hotel without a fight."

"Probably not," Lee agreed, and it fell silent as we all thought on that.

An idea suddenly occurred to me. And, the more I thought on it, the more I liked it.

"I'd like to ride into town alone tomorrow," I announced.

"What for?" Lee looked at me.

"Want to try something."

"What if it doesn't work?"

"Then April might have to be disappointed."

"While you're in town, what do *we* do?" Lee asked.

"Not much," I replied. "Smoke a few cigars, mebbe drink some coffee."

Lee looked thoughtful.

"So, in other words," he said. "You want us to do nothing while you go solve everything."

"Pretty much."

Lee frowned his displeasure.

"But I wanted to show April that *I* could handle things, not you," he objected.

"We can tell her it was *all* your idea."

Lee's face lit up.

"You'd do that for me?"

"Only if it works."

Lee thought it over and nodded slowly.

"All right," he declared. "We'll do our part."

"I knew I could depend on you," I said wryly.

Chapter fifty-nine

We mounted up and rode out a few hours before daylight. It was a cool morning, and we trotted briskly.

We pulled up about a mile from town. We dismounted, and I readjusted the packhorses and looked at Lee and Brian.

"I'll need the contract," I said.

They glanced at each other, and then Brian reached inside his pocket, pulled it out, and handed it to me.

"Don't lose it," Lee said.

"I won't," I said, and added, "Give me a few hours."

Lee nodded.

"We'll wait here."

I returned the nod, and then I tied Clint's horse's lead rope to Gage's saddle.

I nodded goodbye to Lee and Brian, stepped into the saddle, and nudged Little Man forward. Gage and Clint's horse fell in behind, and we trotted to town.

I spotted Ross sitting on the porch at the sheriff's office. He was drinking coffee and studying a chessboard.

He looked up and spotted me. A wry smile split his lips as he studied my packhorses.

A crowd gathered as I pulled up at the jail. The three city council members were present, and I grunted my pleasure.

Everyone stared at the packhorses. The bodies were still wrapped in the tarps, so nobody knew who they were.

"You've been busy," Ross noted.

I started to reply, but I stopped myself just in time.

I dismounted and said, "Just a touch."

Fred Stilwell pushed his way through the crowd. He eyed the packhorses, and then he turned to me.

"Is that Lee and Brian?" He asked.

"Nope," I replied.

"Who is it then?" Fred demanded.

"Gage and Clint Palmer," I announced.

"Who's that?" Fred looked confused.

"The fellers that robbed the hotel," I explained.

A surprised murmur passed through the crowd, and Fred scowled his displeasure.

"But Ed said-," he started to say.

"Ed was wrong," I interrupted, and I raised my voice so everyone could hear. "Lee and Brian had nothing to do with robbing the hotel. Everyone understand that?"

Everybody nodded, and I looked sternly at the city council members.

"And don't forget it," I warned.

"We won't," Morgan spoke up.

"Good," I said, and I glanced at Fred and gestured at the packhorses. "I've got some business to attend to. You take care of *them*."

Fred didn't like that, but I turned away before he could protest. I tied Little Man to a hitching post and walked toward the hotel.

Chapter sixty

The Tobacco Cousins, as Lee and Brian called them, were watching things from the porch of the hotel. They eyed me curiously as I approached, but I ignored them. I stepped up onto the porch, pushed through the batwing doors, and walked into the lobby.

The bartender's face sharpened in curiosity when he spotted me.

"Help you?" He asked.

"Ed in the office?" I asked.

"He is, but he's busy."

I nodded and walked toward the back.

"I said he's busy," the bartender called after me.

"I heard you," I said, and kept going.

I walked to the door, knocked, and opened it abruptly.

Ed was seated behind the desk, shuffling through some papers. He glanced up irritably, but his expression changed when he recognized me.

"Sheriff," he said, surprised. "What are you doing here?"

I shut the door, walked over to his desk, and sat. Ed just stared at me with his mouth open, exposing his upper teeth even more.

"We should talk," I said.

"More questions?" He asked.

"The men who robbed the hotel," I said plainly. "They're dead. I killed them."

A pleased look crossed Ed's face.

"Good!" He exclaimed. "And the money?"

"It's been recovered."

Ed clapped his hands together in glee.

"Great job, Sheriff! I knew you could handle it."

I ignored the praise.

"Ed," I said.

"Yes, Sheriff?"

"You lied to me."

Ed was startled. He started to laugh, then stopped.

"I beg your pardon?"

"Lee and Brian didn't rob the hotel," I said.

A patient look crossed Ed's face.

"But I saw Lee," he reminded. "He's the one who hit me."

"You were mistaken."

We looked at each other a moment. Then Ed forced a smile and tried to recover.

"Well, it is possible I made a mistake," he laughed shakily. "Everything happened so fast, and I *was* very dizzy."

"No, you lied about it," I said bluntly.

"Now, look here, Sheriff-."

"You wanted me to take care of Lee and Brian," I accused. "Meanwhile, you sent Curt and Rod after Gage and Clint."

"Who's Gage and Clint?" Ed tried to look ignorant.

"The fellers that robbed the hotel," I informed.

Ed didn't reply, and a heavy silence filled the room. Several seconds passed, and Ed swallowed and tried to look pleasant.

"Well, like I said," he said. "It's possible I made a mistake. However, what really matters is that you caught the men responsible."

I smiled at that, reached inside my pocket, and pulled out the contract.

Ed watched my every move, and he narrowed his eyes warily.

"Recognize this?" I waved the paper at him.

"I'm afraid I don't," he shook his head.

"This contract was in the safe," I informed. "It says Lee, Brian, and the late Jeremiah Wisdom are the owners of the hotel."

"That was an old agreement," Ed said. "Jeremiah and I became partners later."

"So *you* say," I said, and I smiled as I recalled Lee's words. "I assume you have proof?"

"Proof?" Ed scowled.

I nodded.

"Legal documentation of any kind?"

"Well, I-," he stammered.

"Without proof, the hotel belongs to Lee and Brian," I said. "And, so does the contents in the safe."

Ed stared at me, and my smile never wavered.

"You can't do this," he objected.

"Actually, I can."

"This is ridiculous. Any court of law will side with me."

I leaned forward in my chair and thrust out my jaw.

"Around here," I said softly, "I *am* the law."

Ed started to say something, then stopped. We looked at each other some more, and several seconds passed.

"Just try and force me out," he warned. "I'll fight, and I've got the men to do it."

"About that," I replied. "Curt and Rod don't work for you anymore."

"What?"

"We explained the situation," I said. "They thought it over, and decided to ride on."

Ed scowled at that.

"No matter," he replied. "I still have Chewy and Quirley."

"Yes, we can't forget about them," I agreed, and asked, "I wonder what'll happen when they learn you're broke?"

Ed snorted.

"I have money," he said.

"Then you'd better pay them," I suggested, "because they're going to earn it."

Ed's scowl deepened. He didn't say anything, and I stood and started for the door.

"Where you going?" Ed wanted to know.

"To talk to Chewy and Quirley," I replied.

"Hold on now, *please*," Ed's expression suddenly changed. "I haven't paid them anything. They'll kill me."

"You just said you had money," I reminded.

Ed didn't reply, and I nodded knowingly.

"Another lie," I said. "Now, ain't that just *too* bad."

"Can't we work something out?" Ed looked desperate.

I stood there and looked at him. He looked pitiful, but I didn't feel sorry for him.

"I'll wait an hour," I said. "That should give you enough time to get out of town."

"But they'll come after me!" Ed protested.

"Then you'd best hurry," I suggested.

Before Ed could reply, I turned, opened the door, and walked out.

Epilogue

Ross and I sat on the porch at the jail, drinking coffee and playing chess.

Ross was in a good mood as he studied the chessboard.

"I talked to the city council," he said. "Told them I was quitting."

"How'd they take it?" I asked.

"They were real polite and respectful," Ross replied. "But, I could tell they were happy to have you back."

"We'll see about that," I said.

"Soon as I quit, I felt all happy and excited," Ross continued. "I'm ready to move on, and see what's out there."

"I'm glad to hear you say that," I said earnestly.

"When do you figure on leaving for Midway?" Ross asked as he moved.

"A day or two," I replied as I squinted at the chessboard. "I want to spend some time with Rachel first."

"I'll be ready, soon as you are."

"I'll let you know," I said, and then I moved my queen. "Checkmate."

Ross uttered a gasp of surprise, and he scowled as he studied his position. I smiled and looked up the street.

"Here comes Lee and Brian," I announced.

Ross muttered to himself as he looked up, and we watched as they rode up and pulled up in front of us.

They seemed uneasy. Lee glanced up and down the street, and then he looked at me.

"Are we still wanted, notorious outlaws?" He asked.

"Not at the moment," I replied.

"The town knows?"

"They know," I nodded.

They looked relieved. Lee glanced at the hotel, and asked, "Where's Ed?"

"He left town," I said, and added, "So did the Tobacco Cousins."

"What happened?" Lee looked startled.

"I reasoned with him."

"Reasoned?" Lee made a face.

"Sure," I nodded. "And, about an hour later, I informed the Tobacco Cousins that their boss couldn't pay up and had left town."

"How'd they take the news?"

"Seemed mighty upset," I replied. "They gathered their belongings and left in a hurry."

Lee and Brian looked pleased. They glanced at each other and grinned.

"Do you think the Tobacco Cousins will catch Ed?" Ross spoke up.

"Might," I said.

"They'll kill him," Ross pointed out.

"Might," I said again.

Ross frowned at me.

"You're fine with that?"

"Yes," I said truthfully. "I think I am."

"Don't worry, Ross," Lee spoke up. "Fellers like Ed always seem to land on their feet. I'm sure he'll survive."

"That's the only thing that worries me," I said.

"What's that?" Lee looked at me.

"Ed isn't the sort to forget," I explained. "He'll hold a grudge."

Lee thought on that and shrugged.

"I can live with that," he said.

"Time will tell," I replied, and I stood and looked at Ross. "Well, talk to you later."

"Going somewhere?" Ross asked.

"Yep," I said, and I walked over to Little Man and untied him. Then I looked at Lee and Brian and asked, "You coming, or do you need to attend to the hotel?"

"Hotel can wait," Lee grinned.

"Anxious to see someone?" I smiled.

"Reckon I am," Lee returned the smile.

"Me too," I admitted.

I stepped in the saddle and kicked Little Man forward. Lee and Brian fell in beside me, and we trotted down the main street.

We rode by our house, and I pulled up and looked the place over.

The door had been repaired, and the windowpane replaced. The new paint job was also finished and looked great.

I smiled as I thought of us living there. I pictured Rachel standing in the doorway, waving me off to work, and a little youngster clinging to her leg, peeking around her apron at me.

"What are you smiling at?" Lee interrupted my thoughts.

"Nothing much," I replied.

In my moment of bliss, I forgot about Little Man.

As soon as those words left my mouth, he exploded. He shot up straight in the air, hit the ground hard, and bucked forward.

I was surprised, but I managed to stay on.

He took several more big jumps, and I was thrown forward in the saddle. Then he sucked backwards, and I did a flip in the air and landed hard.

I gasped for air while the dust settled. Meanwhile, Lee and Brian tried not to laugh.

I groaned, sat up slowly, and glared at Little Man, who was just standing there looking disinterested.

"You're right," Lee said with a straight face. "You can't ride him."

I ignored Lee as I climbed to my feet.

"I'll be back," I said, and I limped down the street and walked into Morgan's saloon.

Morgan was behind the bar, and he was surprised to see me.

"Help you, Sheriff?" He asked.

"I need a bottle of whiskey," I announced.

Morgan was surprised.

"I didn't know you were a drinking man."

"I'm not," I said. "It's for my horse."

Morgan took my money and asked no more questions.

Ear problems are extremely rare with horses. However, middle ear infections *can* happen. It is a result of bacterial infections that come from the bloodstream.

Side effects include ear rubbing and head tossing. A severely affected horse can be highly agitated at times, have sensitive hearing, and... will buck often.

About the Author

Born in West Texas, Tell Cotten is a seventh generation Texan. He comes from a family with a ranching heritage and is a member of the Sons of the Republic of Texas. Besides writing, he is also in the cattle business, and he resides in West Texas with his wife, Andi, and their two children.

Tell has enjoyed writing from an early age, and he also has a great love of the history of the west. FASTEST GUN AROUND is his ninth novel in The Landon Saga series.

For announcements of new releases and all other information, please like The Landon Saga Page on Facebook https://www.facebook.com/TheLandonSaga
Or, you can join The Landon Saga Fan Group
https://www.facebook.com/groups/784798154926122/
You can also visit Tell Cotten's website
http://tellcotten.wordpress.com/

Acknowledgements

I would like to thank my wife and my family for all their help and support. Without them this wouldn't be possible. I'd also like to thank God for the gift of writing.

Special thanks goes out to Bill for the fantastic drawing, and thanks to Mike and Marcy for putting the cover together.

And lastly, I'd like to thank Melissa for all her advice, help, and hard work.

Enjoy this excerpt from Tell Cotten's upcoming novel:

Midway
Book ten in The Landon Saga series

Whenever Yancy and I were in town, our morning routine was to make another pot of coffee after breakfast, sit out on the porch, and watch the sun come up.

This morning was no different.

Yancy placed a fresh pot of coffee on a small table between us. He sat, poured us both a cup, added three spoonfuls of sugar to his, and stirred. Then we picked up our cups, took deep swigs, and sighed in contentment.

"Good coffee," Yancy remarked.

"Nobody makes it like you," I replied.

"Josie can't?"

"No," I said truthfully. "She can't."

"Coop, have you tried teaching her?"

"Some."

"And?" Yancy prompted.

"It's worse now than it was."

The thought of burned coffee was almost more than Yancy could tolerate. He shook his head slowly and looked sympathetic.

"I'm sorry," he said, and added, "But, *you* married her."

"What was I thinking," I said wryly. A few seconds passed, and I asked, "Can Jessica make coffee?"

A worried look crossed Yancy's face.

"You know, I'm not exactly sure."

"Too late now," I said.

Yancy didn't reply, and I chuckled and took another swig.

After that we just sat there, and neither one of us spoke. There was nothing uncomfortable with the silence; that's just how it was with Yancy and me.

"Hard to believe," I finally said.

Yancy looked at me.

"What is?"

"My little brother, getting married today."

"Had to happen sometime," Yancy replied.

"I wasn't so sure," I said, and I grinned when Yancy scowled at me. "I'm real happy for you, Yancy," I added earnestly. "And for Jessica."

"Thank you, Coop."

"Are you sure you can handle married life?"

"You seem to be doing just fine."

"But Josie ain't like most women," I pointed out.

"Neither is Jessica."

"True, but Jessica is a sensitive lady," I warned. "She has feelings, and she lets them be known. Now take Josie; she doesn't express her feelings so much."

"She seemed mighty upset when we disliked her cooking," Yancy reminded.

"Cooking aside, she's a pretty tough gal."

"So what's your point?"

I thought on that and frowned.

"Well, I'm not exactly sure now," I admitted.

Yancy started to reply, but stopped. He was looking down the street, and a curious look crossed his face.

I turned and looked.

Three Mexican men were riding into town. They were travel worn, covered in dust, and in need of a bath and shave. They all displayed Colts on their hips, and they had a hard look about them.

"Ever see them before?" Yancy asked.

"Not that I can recall," I shook my head.

"They look like trouble."

"Do," I agreed.

"I don't like it."

"Neither do I," I said.

"I wonder who they are."

I started to reply, but stopped myself. I looked at Yancy and frowned.

"Hold it right there," I said sternly.

"What is it?" Yancy looked at me.

"It's your wedding day," I reminded.

"So?"

"You've got better things to do than fret over a few strangers."

"But it's my responsibility," Yancy argued.

"Actually, it's not," I corrected. "Wagons is the sheriff. *We're* Texas Rangers."

Yancy snorted.

"Is that supposed to bring me comfort?"

"Just this once; let it go," I urged. "They're probably just passing through anyway."

"What if they aren't?" Yancy replied. "They could be looking for trouble."

I sighed.

"If it makes you feel better, I'll nose around, ask a few questions," I offered.

Yancy thought it over, then nodded.

"Go ahead and do that."

"Just as soon as I finish my coffee," I suggested.

"Of course," Yancy agreed, and we both took a swig and sighed in contentment.

Coming soon from Solstice Publishing

For announcements of new releases and all other information, please like The Landon Saga Page on Facebook https://www.facebook.com/TheLandonSaga or you can join The Landon Saga Facebook group https://www.facebook.com/groups/784798154926122/